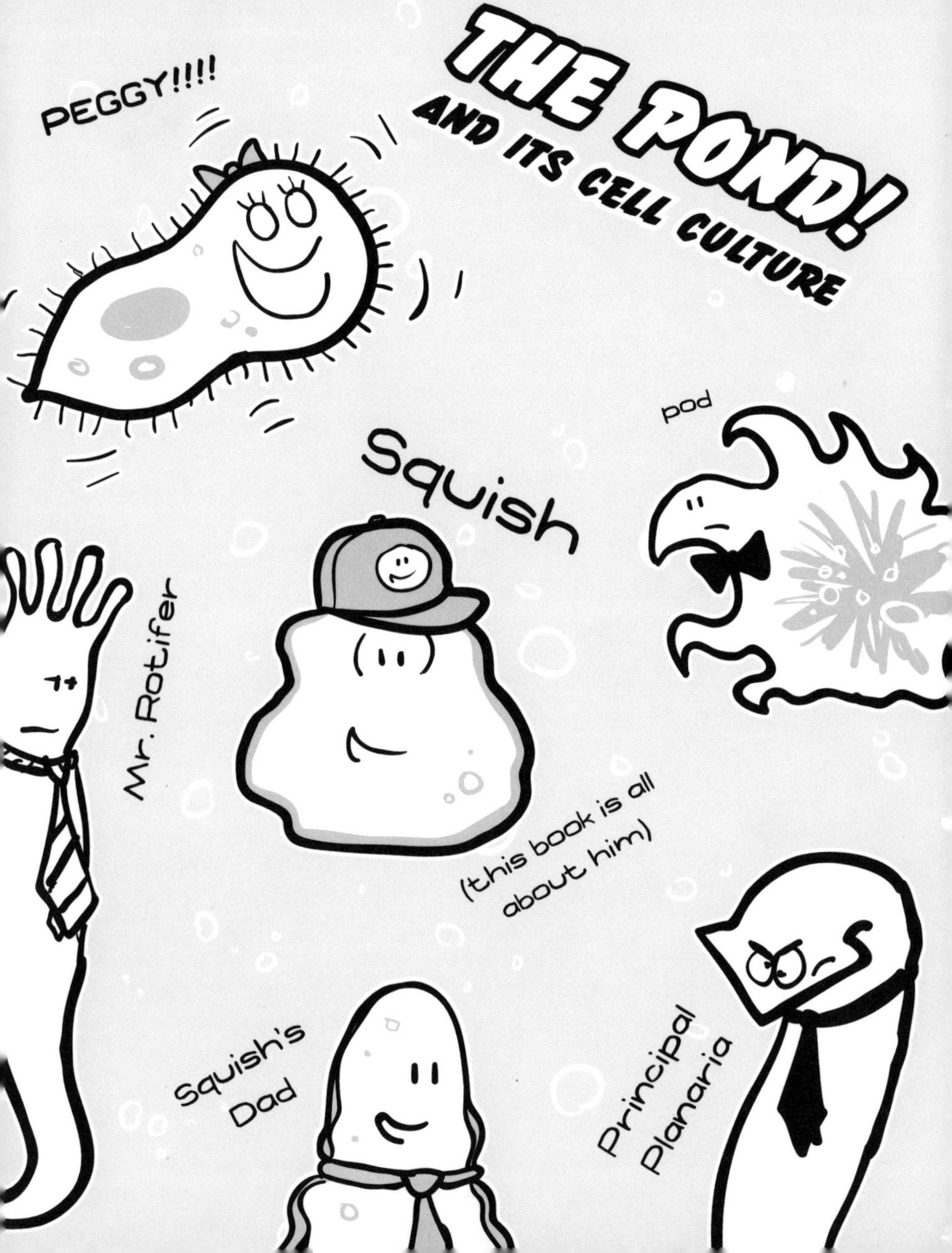
THE POND!
AND ITS CELL CULTURE
PEGGY!!!!
pod
Squish
Mr. Rotifer
(this book is all about him)
Squish's Dad
Principal Planaria

★"HILARIOUS. IF EVER A NEW SERIES DESERVED TO GO VIRAL, THIS ONE DOES."

—KIRKUS REVIEWS, STARRED

Read ALL the SQUISH books!

#1 SQUISH: Super Amoeba
#2 SQUISH: Brave New Pond
#3 SQUISH: The Power of the Parasite
#4 SQUISH: Captain Disaster
#5 SQUISH: Game On!
#6 SQUISH: Fear the Amoeba

squish
FEAR THE AMOEBA

BY JENNIFER L. HOLM & MATTHEW HOLM

RANDOM HOUSE 🏠 NEW YORK

Published in the United States by Random House Children's Books, a division of Random House LLC, a Penguin Random House Company, New York.

Visit us on the Web! randomhouse.com/kids

Educators and librarians, for a variety of teaching tools, visit us at RHTeachersLibrarians.com

Library of Congress Cataloging-in-Publication Data
Holm, Jennifer L.
Fear the amoeba / by Jennifer L. Holm and Matthew Holm. — First edition.
p. cm — (Squish ; 6)
Summary: Afraid to go to horror movies with his friend, Pod, Squish the amoeba feels better after learning that even comic book superheroes get scared sometimes.
ISBN 978-0-307-98302-2 (trade) —
ISBN 978-0-307-98303-9 (lib. bdg.) —
ISBN 978-0-307-98304-6 (ebook)
1. Graphic novels. [1. Graphic novels. 2. Amoeba—Fiction. 3. Fear—Fiction. 4. Horror films—Fiction. 5. Superheroes—Fiction. 6. Cartoons and comics—Fiction.] I. Holm, Matthew. II. Title.
PZ7.7.H65Fe 2014 741.5'973—dc23 2013009098

MANUFACTURED IN MALAYSIA 10 9 8 7 6 5 4 3 2 1
First Edition

Random House Children's Books supports the First Amendment and celebrates the right to read.

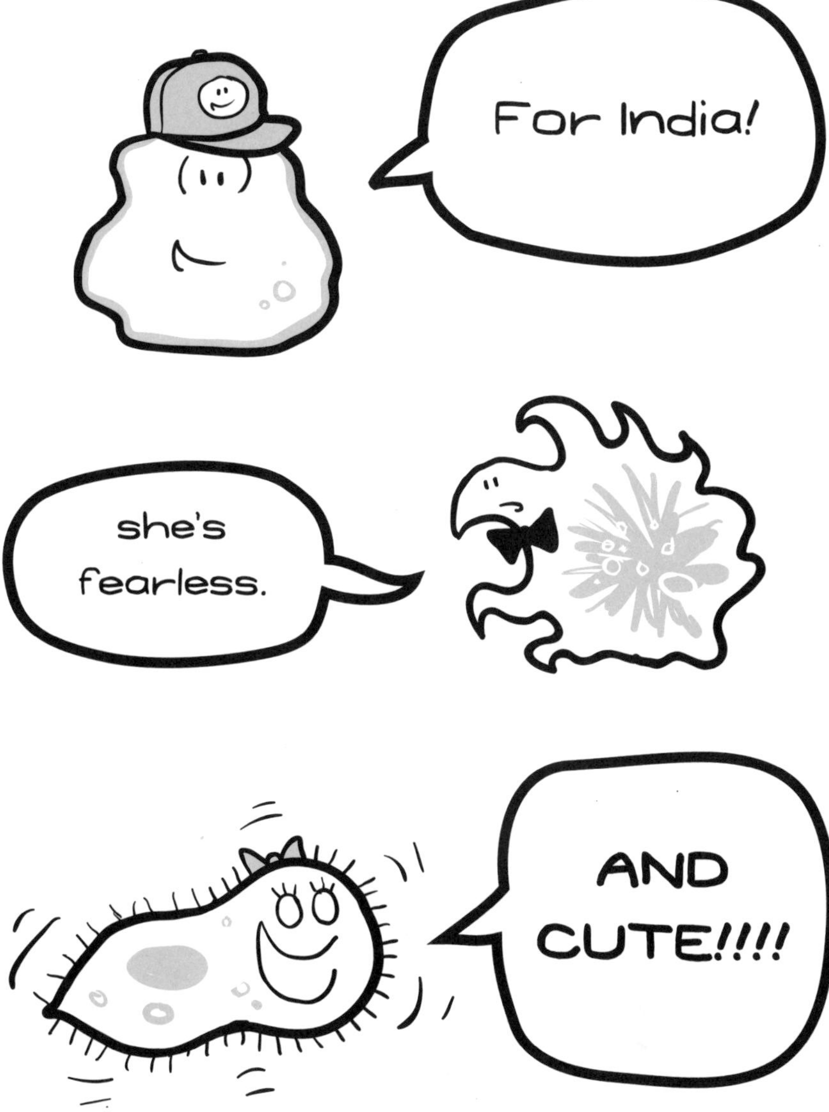
For India!
she's fearless.
AND CUTE!!!!

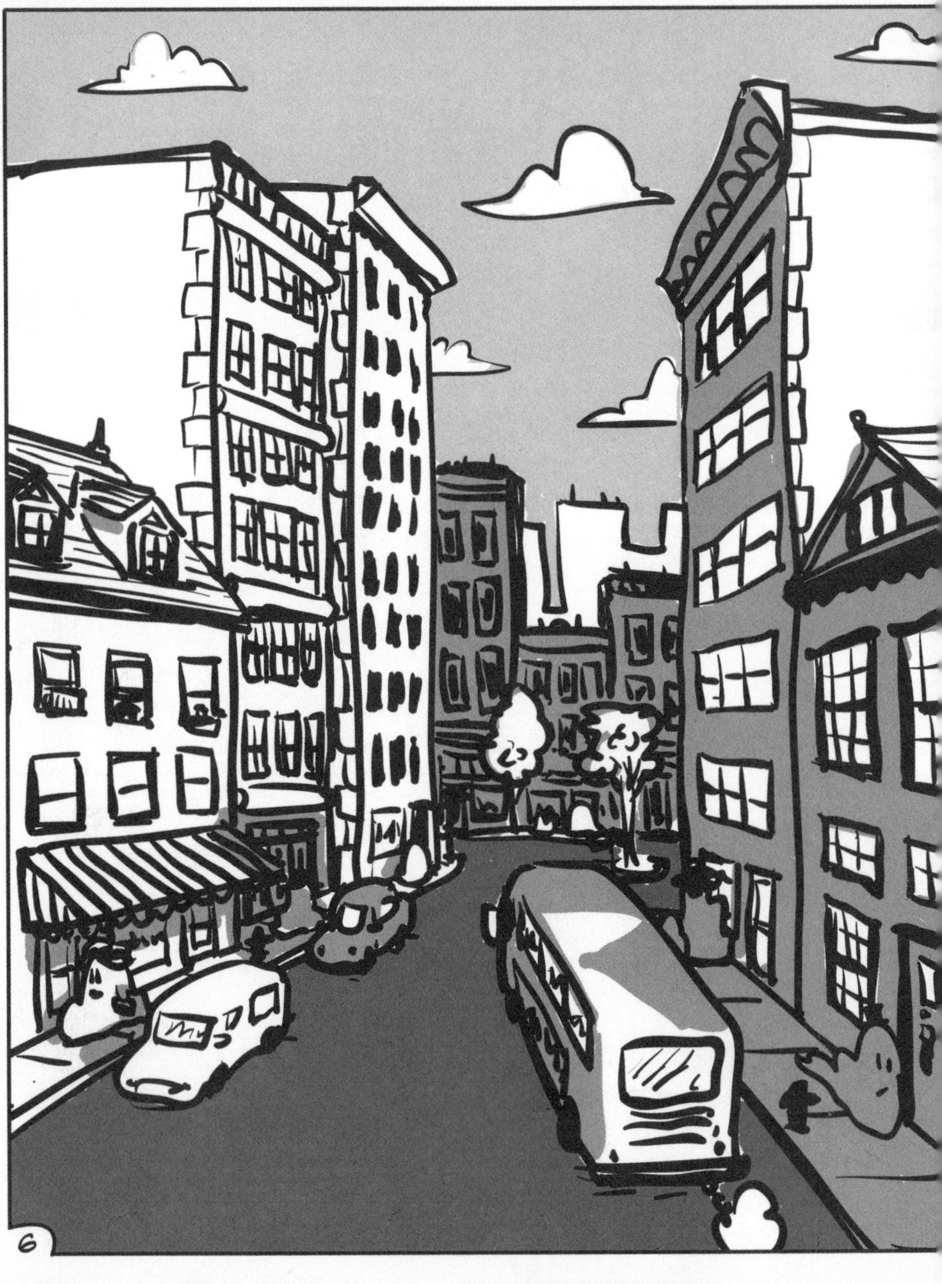

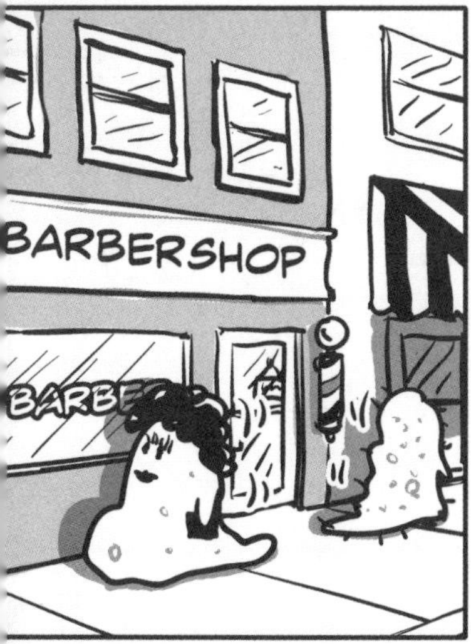
BARBERSHOP

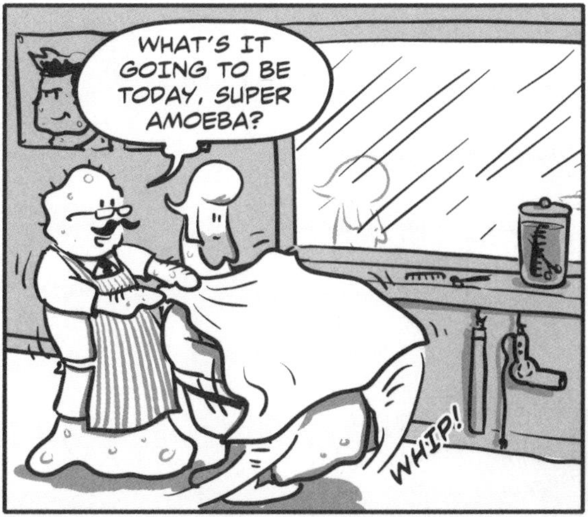
WHAT'S IT GOING TO BE TODAY, SUPER AMOEBA?
WHIP!

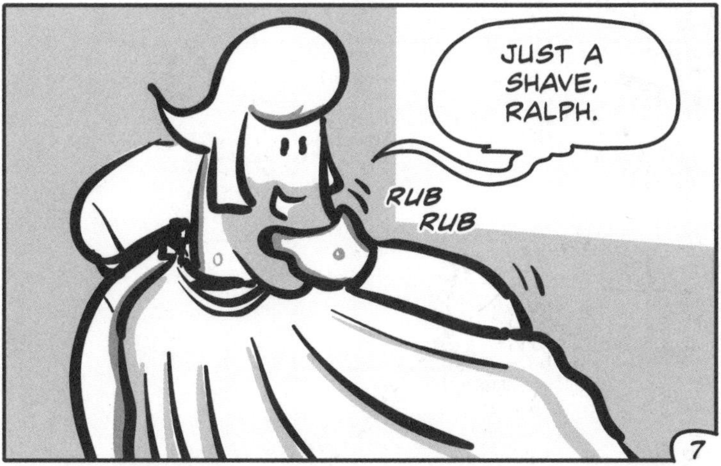
JUST A SHAVE, RALPH.
RUB RUB

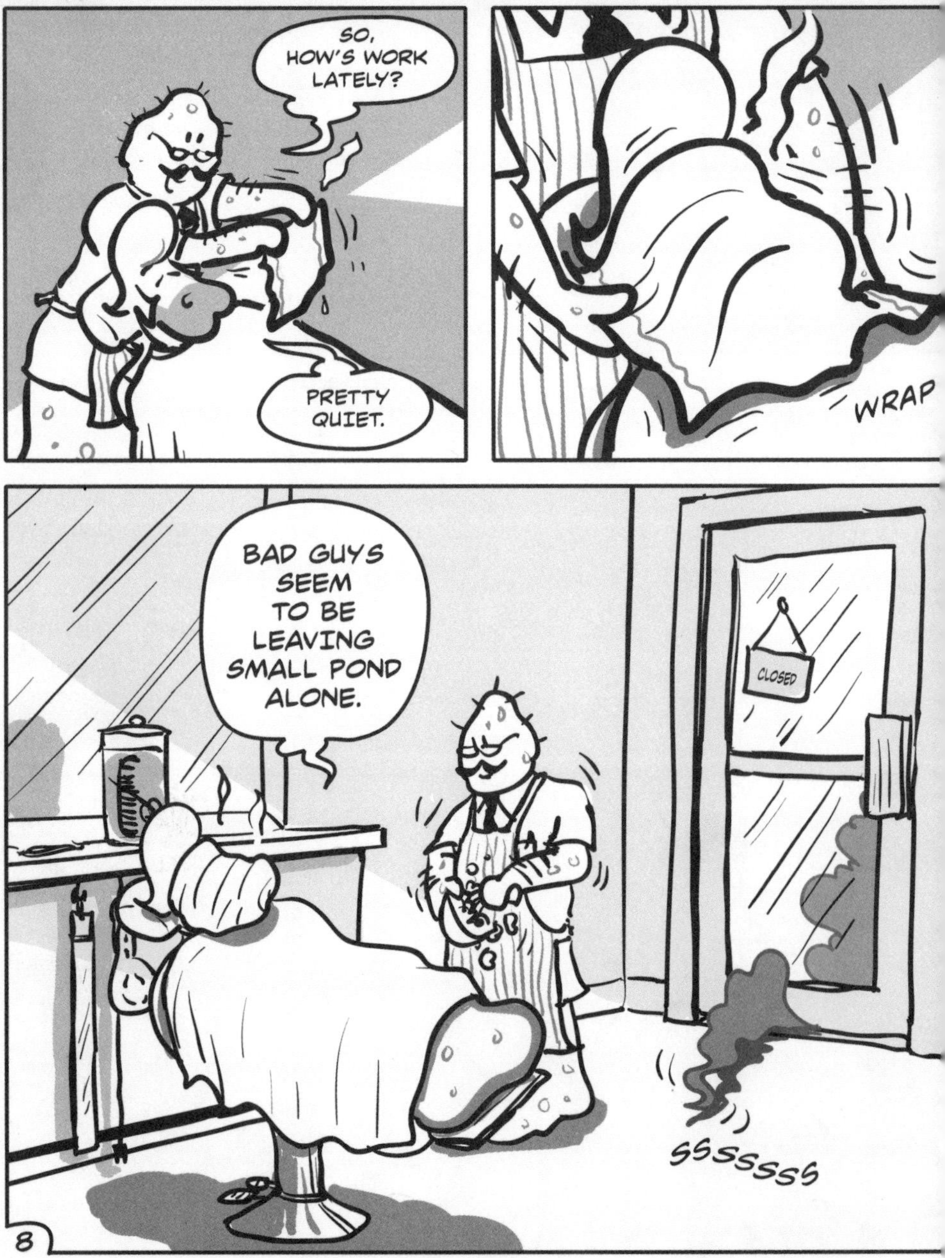
SO, HOW'S WORK LATELY?
PRETTY QUIET.
WRAP
BAD GUYS SEEM TO BE LEAVING SMALL POND ALONE.
CLOSED
SSSSSSS

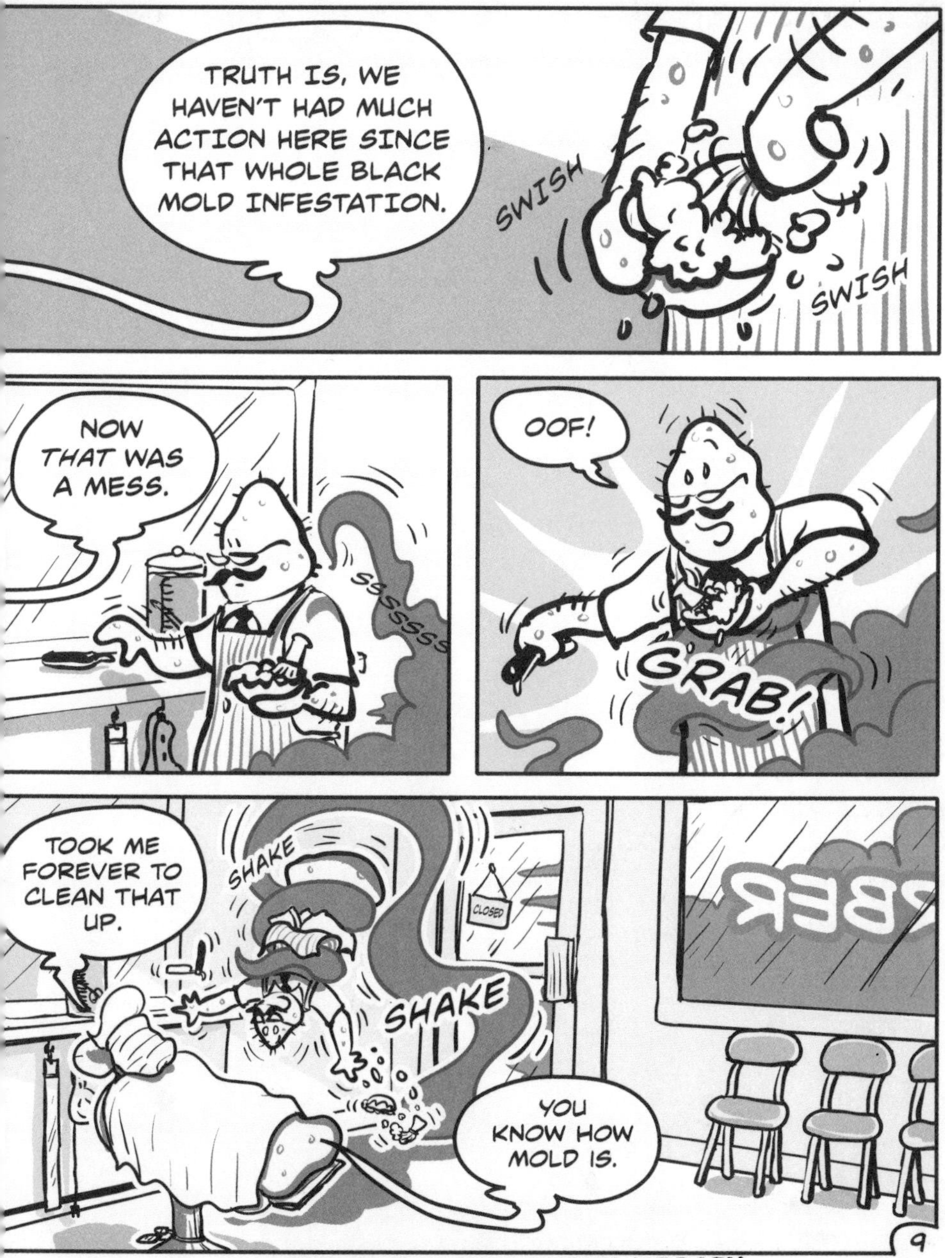

TRUTH IS, WE HAVEN'T HAD MUCH ACTION HERE SINCE THAT WHOLE BLACK MOLD INFESTATION.
SWISH
SWISH
NOW THAT WAS A MESS.
SSSSSSSS
OOF!
GRAB!
TOOK ME FOREVER TO CLEAN THAT UP.
SHAKE
CLOSED
SHAKE
YOU KNOW HOW MOLD IS.

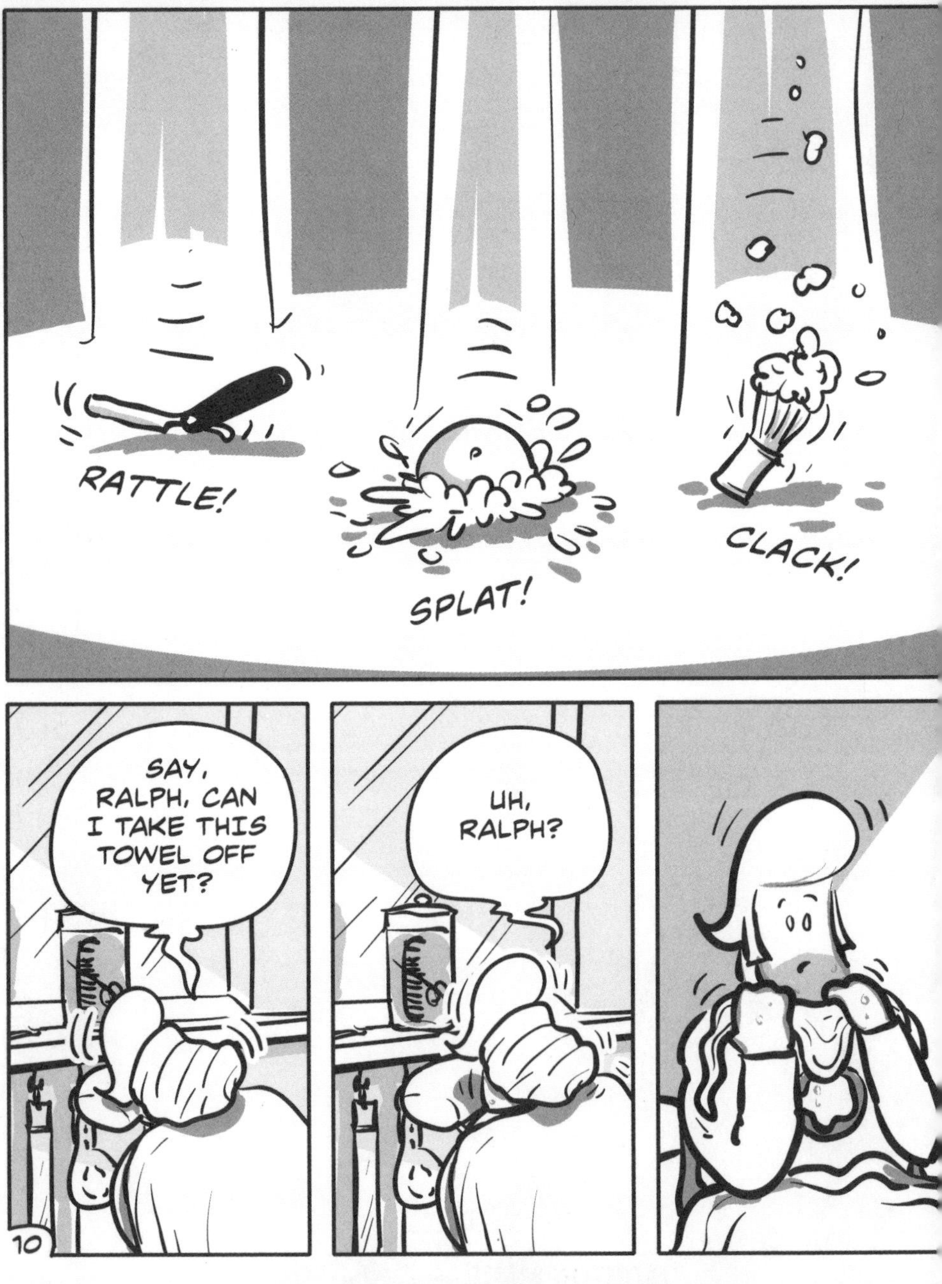
RATTLE!
SPLAT!
CLACK!
SAY, RALPH, CAN I TAKE THIS TOWEL OFF YET?
UH, RALPH?

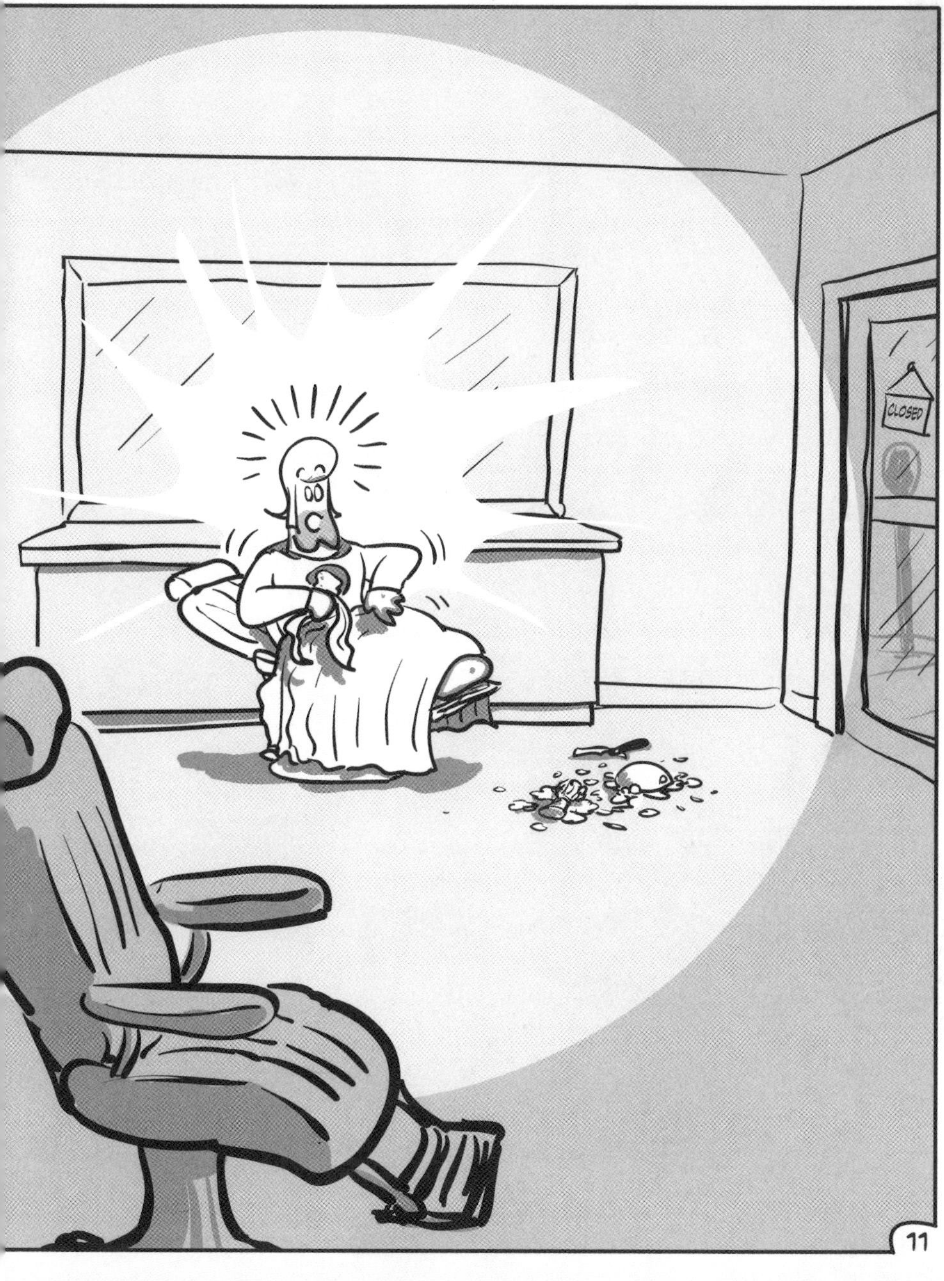
CLOSED

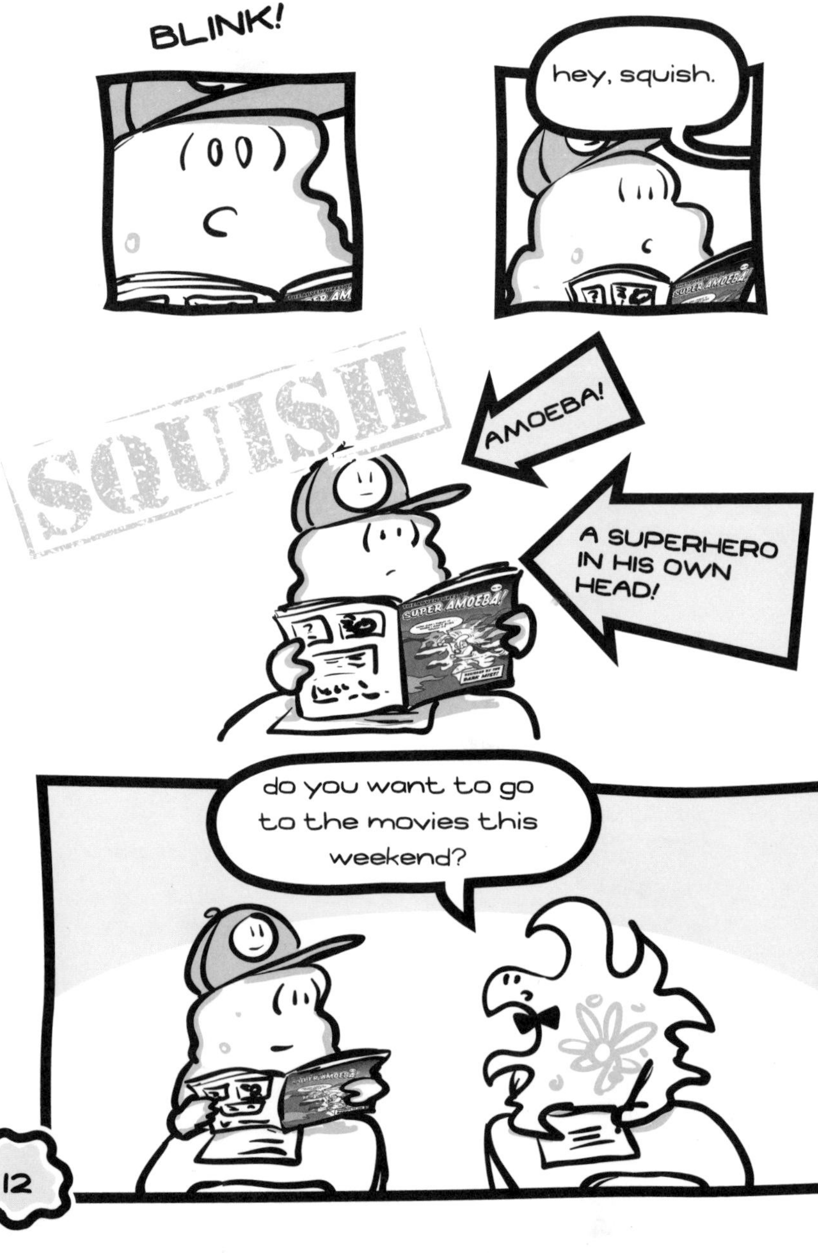
BLINK!
hey, squish.
SQUISH
AMOEBA!
A SUPERHERO IN HIS OWN HEAD!
SUPER AMOEBA!
do you want to go to the movies this weekend?

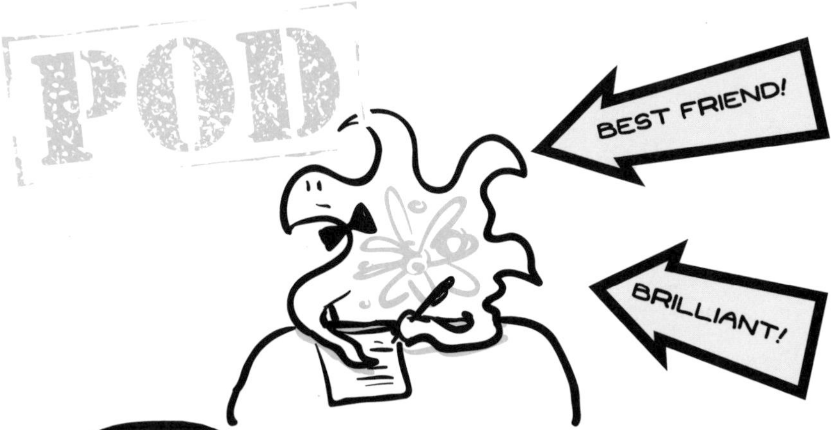
POD
BEST FRIEND!
BRILLIANT!

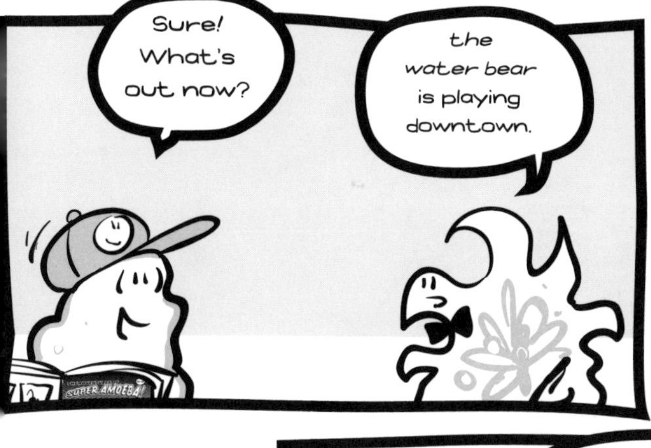
Sure! What's out now?
the *water bear* is playing downtown.
SUPER AMOEBA!

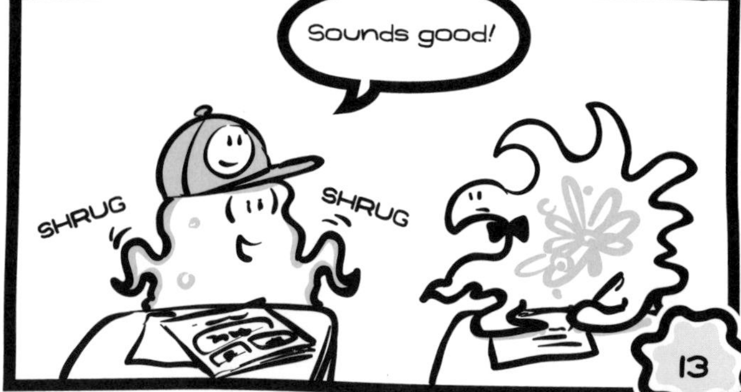
Sounds good!
SHRUG
SHRUG

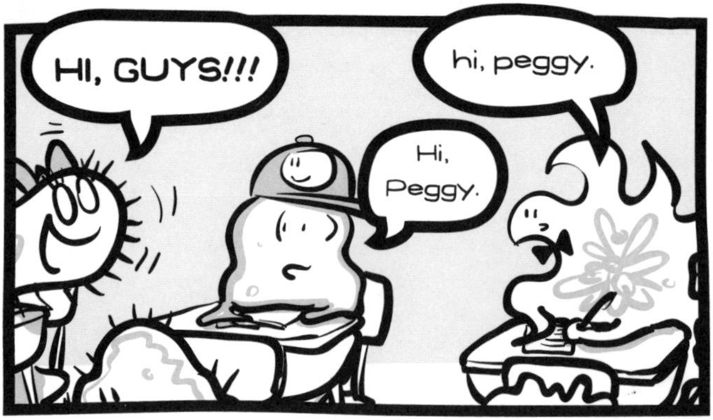
HI, GUYS!!!
hi, peggy.
Hi, Peggy.

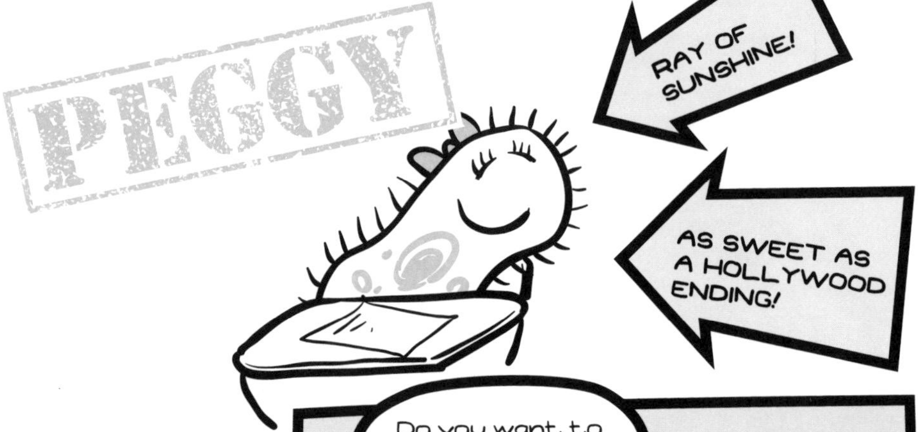
PEGGY
RAY OF SUNSHINE!
AS SWEET AS A HOLLYWOOD ENDING!

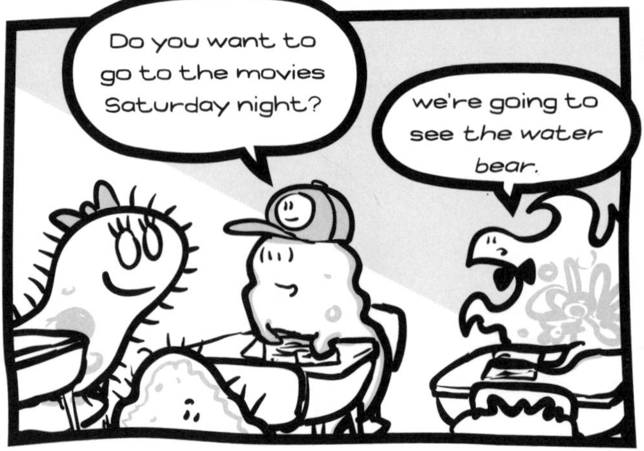
Do you want to go to the movies Saturday night?
we're going to see the water bear.

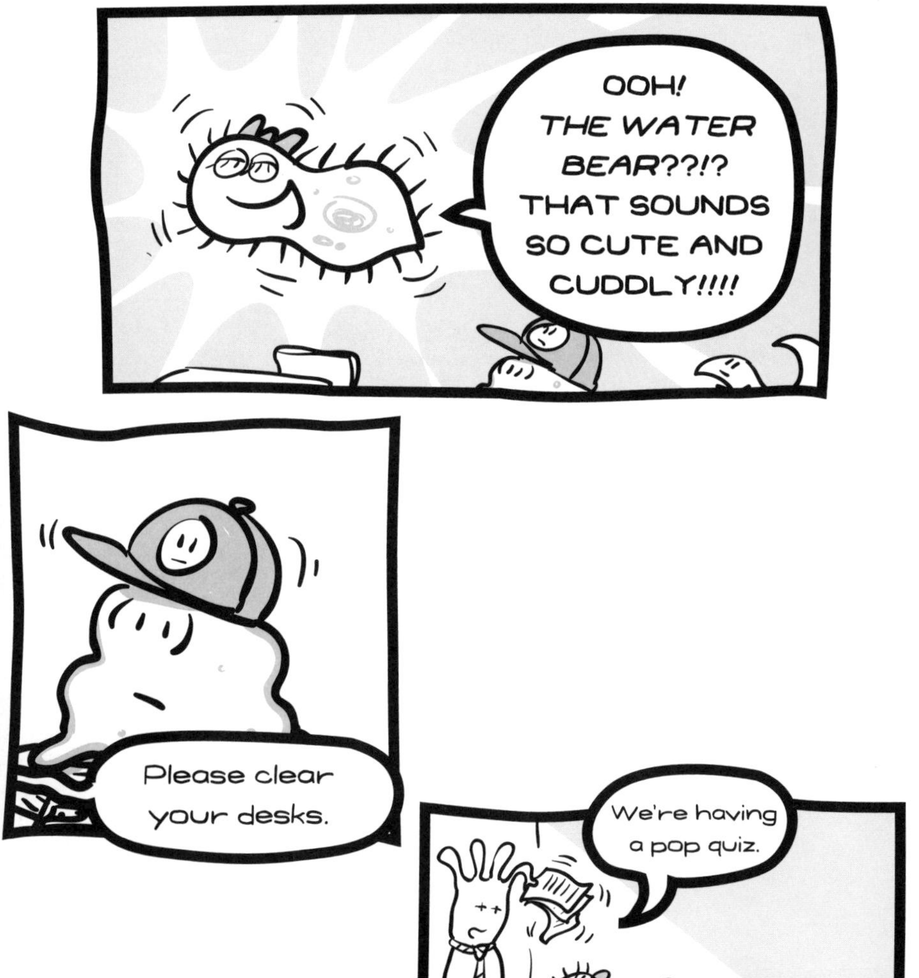
OOH! THE WATER BEAR??!? THAT SOUNDS SO CUTE AND CUDDLY!!!!
Please clear your desks.
We're having a pop quiz.

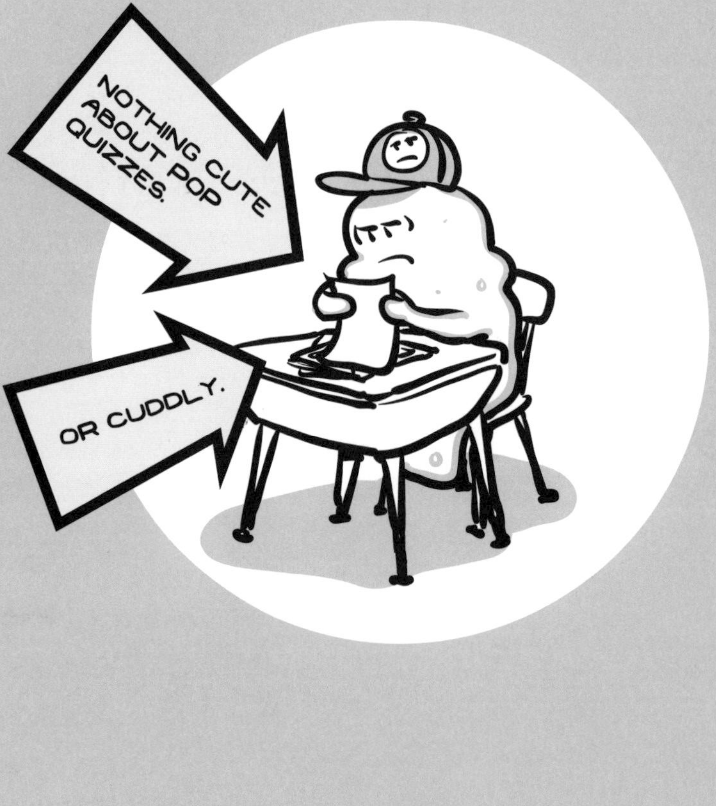
NOTHING CUTE ABOUT POP QUIZZES.
OR CUDDLY.

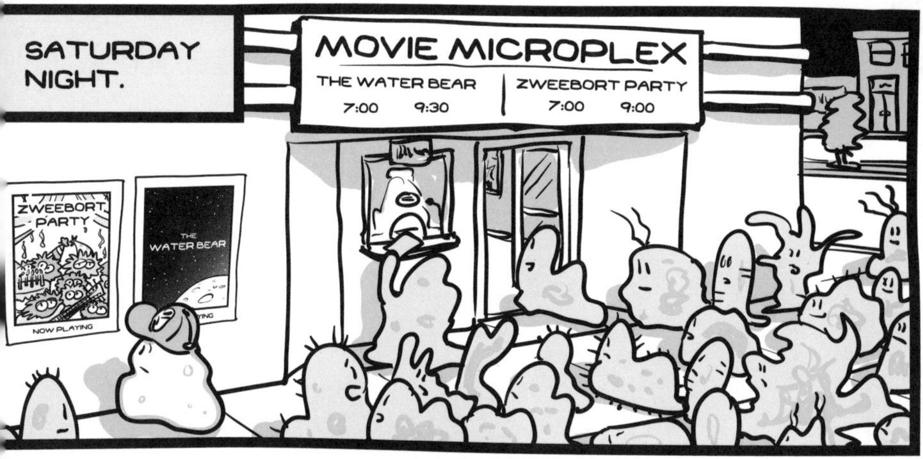
SATURDAY NIGHT.
MOVIE MICROPLEX
THE WATER BEAR
7:00 9:30
ZWEEBORT PARTY
7:00 9:00
ZWEEBORT PARTY
NOW PLAYING
THE WATER BEAR

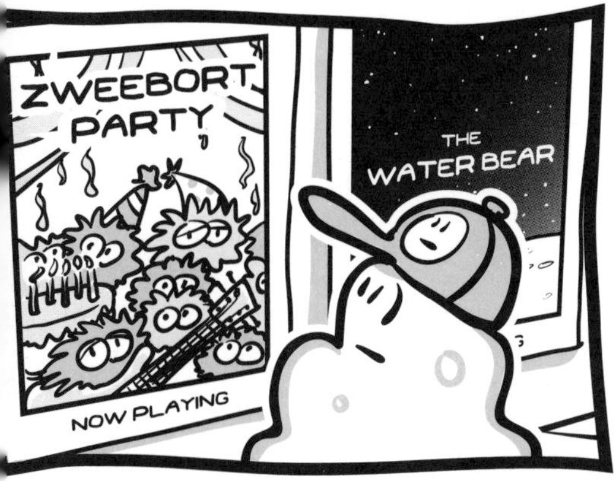
ZWEEBORT PARTY
NOW PLAYING
THE WATER BEAR

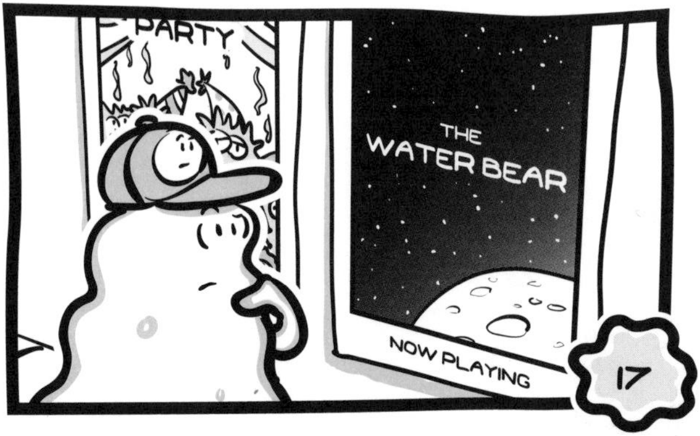
THE WATER BEAR
NOW PLAYING

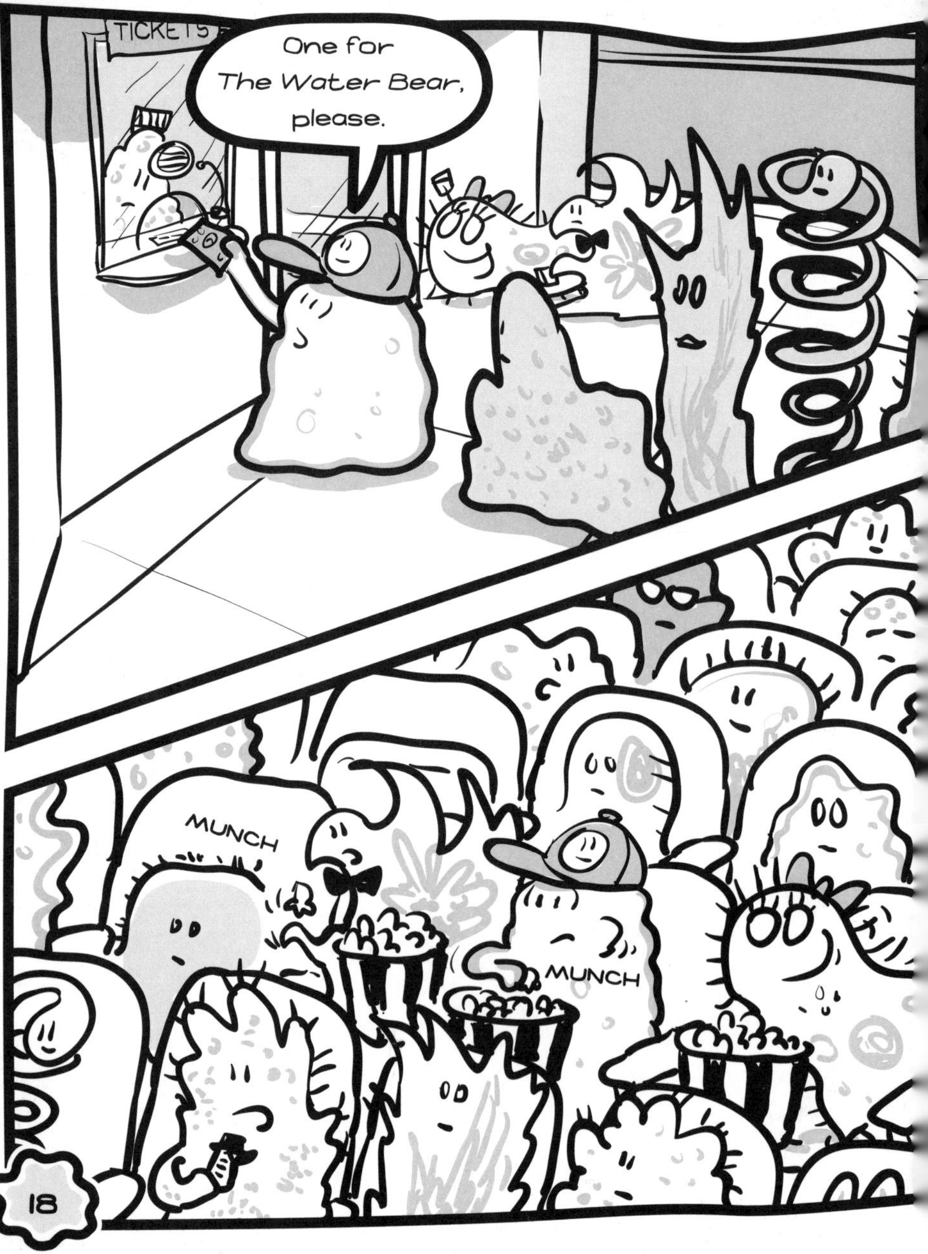
TICKETS
One for The Water Bear, please.
MUNCH
MUNCH

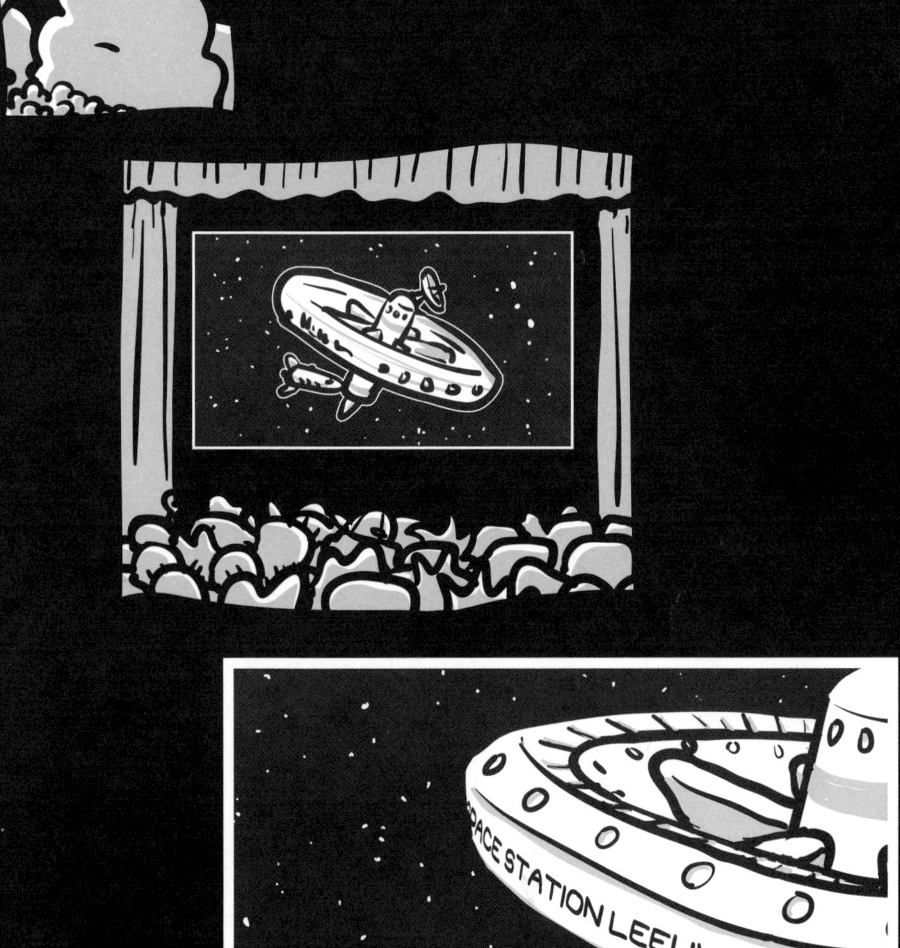
ACE STATION LEEUWENHOEK

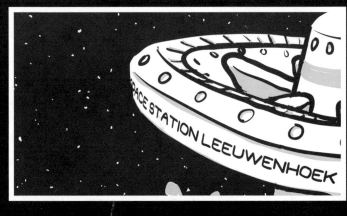

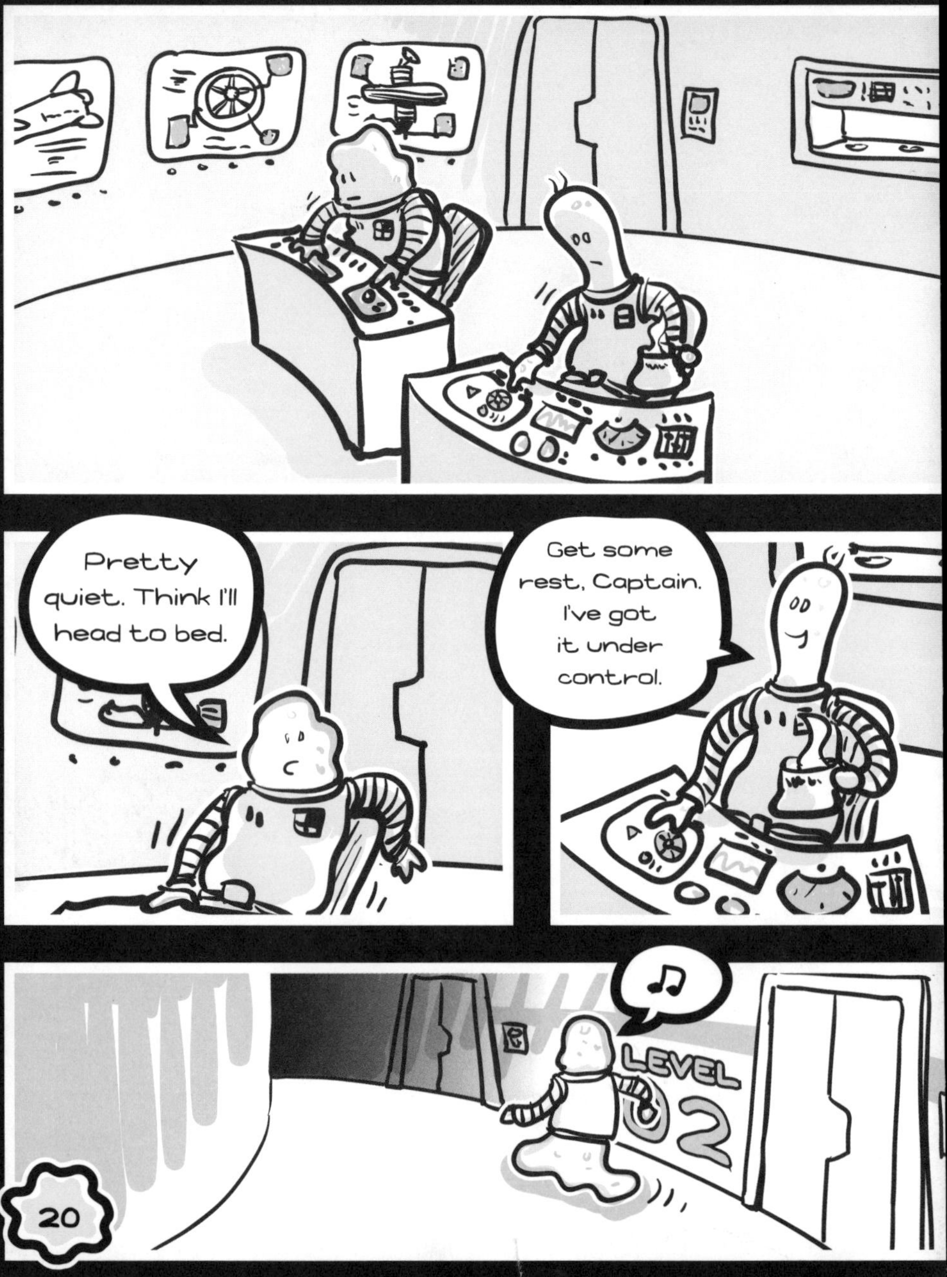
Pretty quiet. Think I'll head to bed.
Get some rest, Captain. I've got it under control.
♫
LEVEL 02

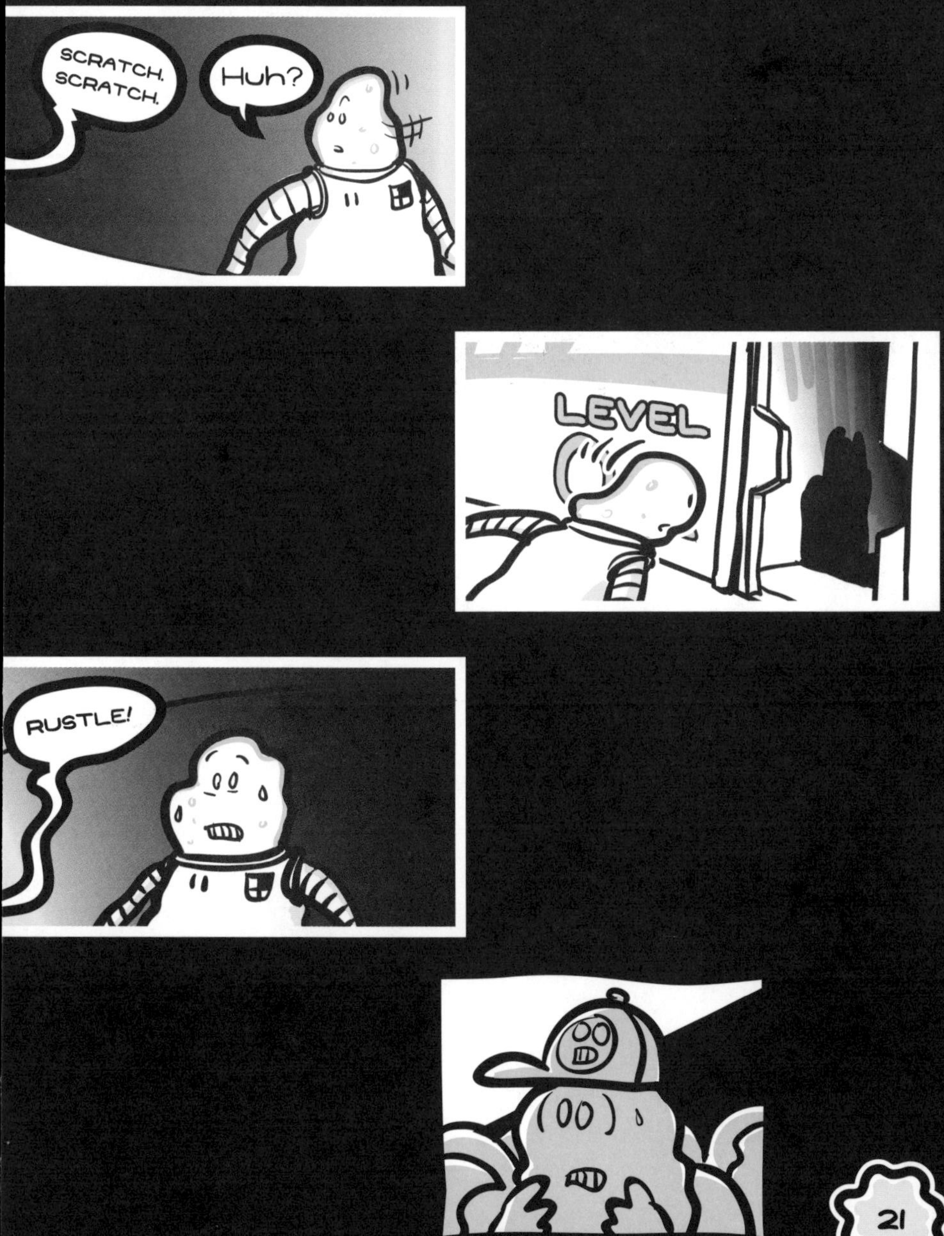
SCRATCH. SCRATCH.
Huh?
LEVEL
RUSTLE!

MEOW!

Whew! Just a kitten.

Ha! Kitten!
HA! HA! HA! HA!

SHIVER

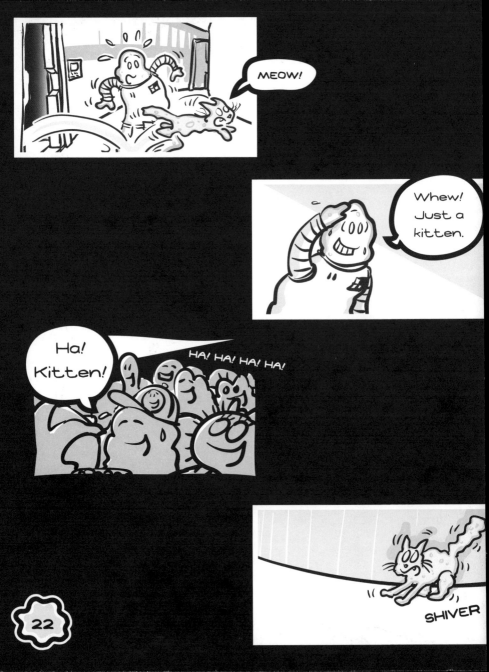

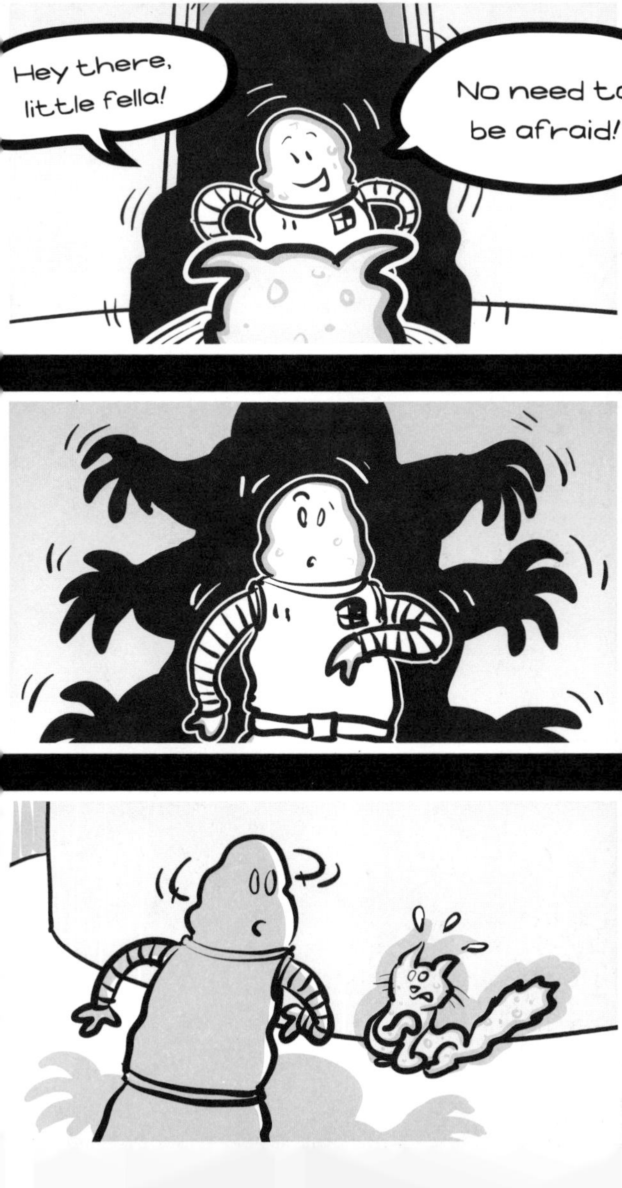
Hey there,
little fella!
No need to
be afraid!

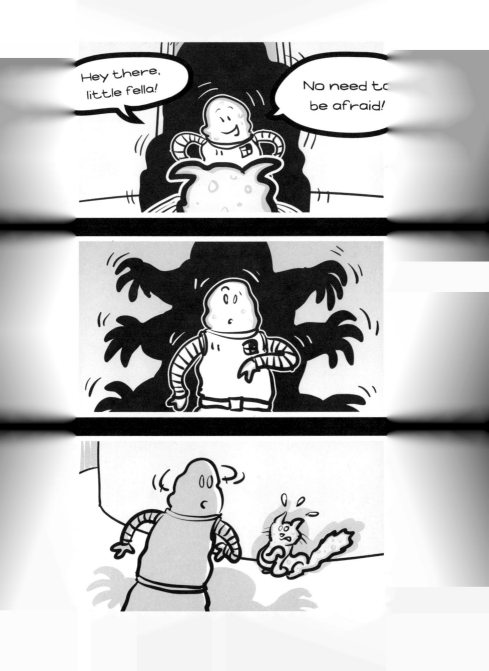

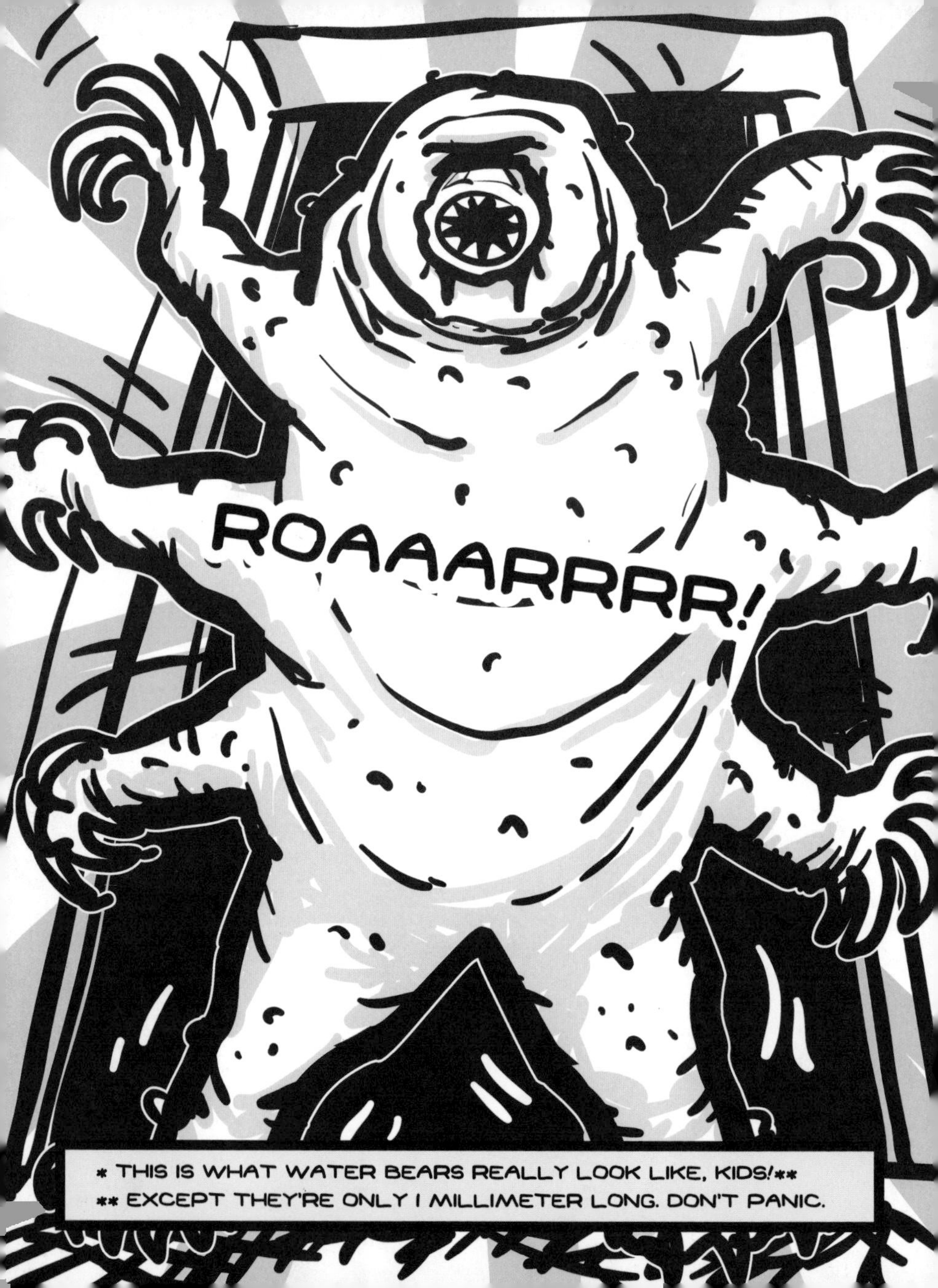
ROAAAARRRRR!
* THIS IS WHAT WATER BEARS REALLY LOOK LIKE, KIDS!**
** EXCEPT THEY'RE ONLY 1 MILLIMETER LONG. DON'T PANIC.

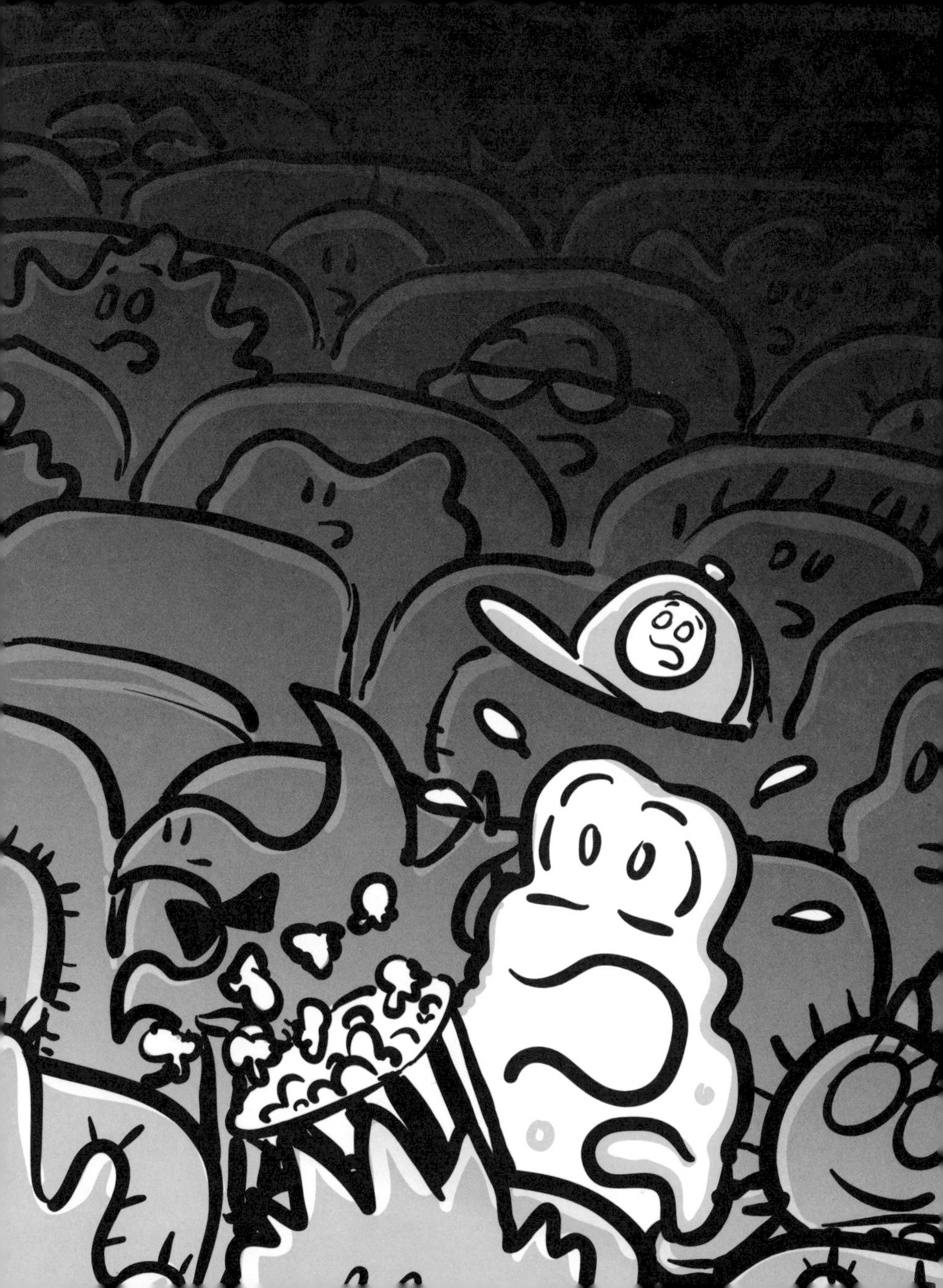

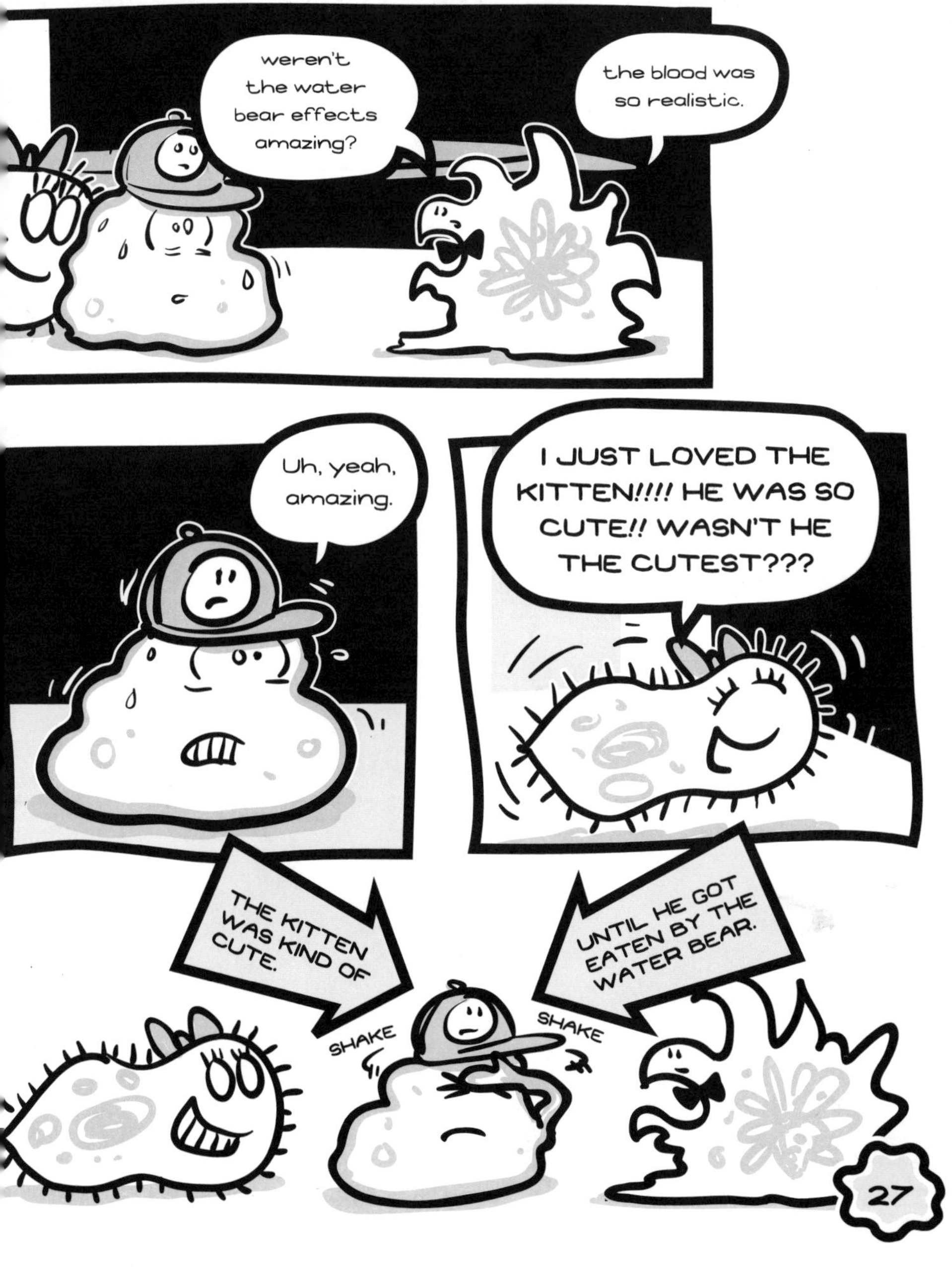
weren't the water bear effects amazing?
the blood was so realistic.
Uh, yeah, amazing.
I JUST LOVED THE KITTEN!!!! HE WAS SO CUTE!! WASN'T HE THE CUTEST???
THE KITTEN WAS KIND OF CUTE.
UNTIL HE GOT EATEN BY THE WATER BEAR.
SHAKE
SHAKE

WHOOOOSH!

WHIP!

29

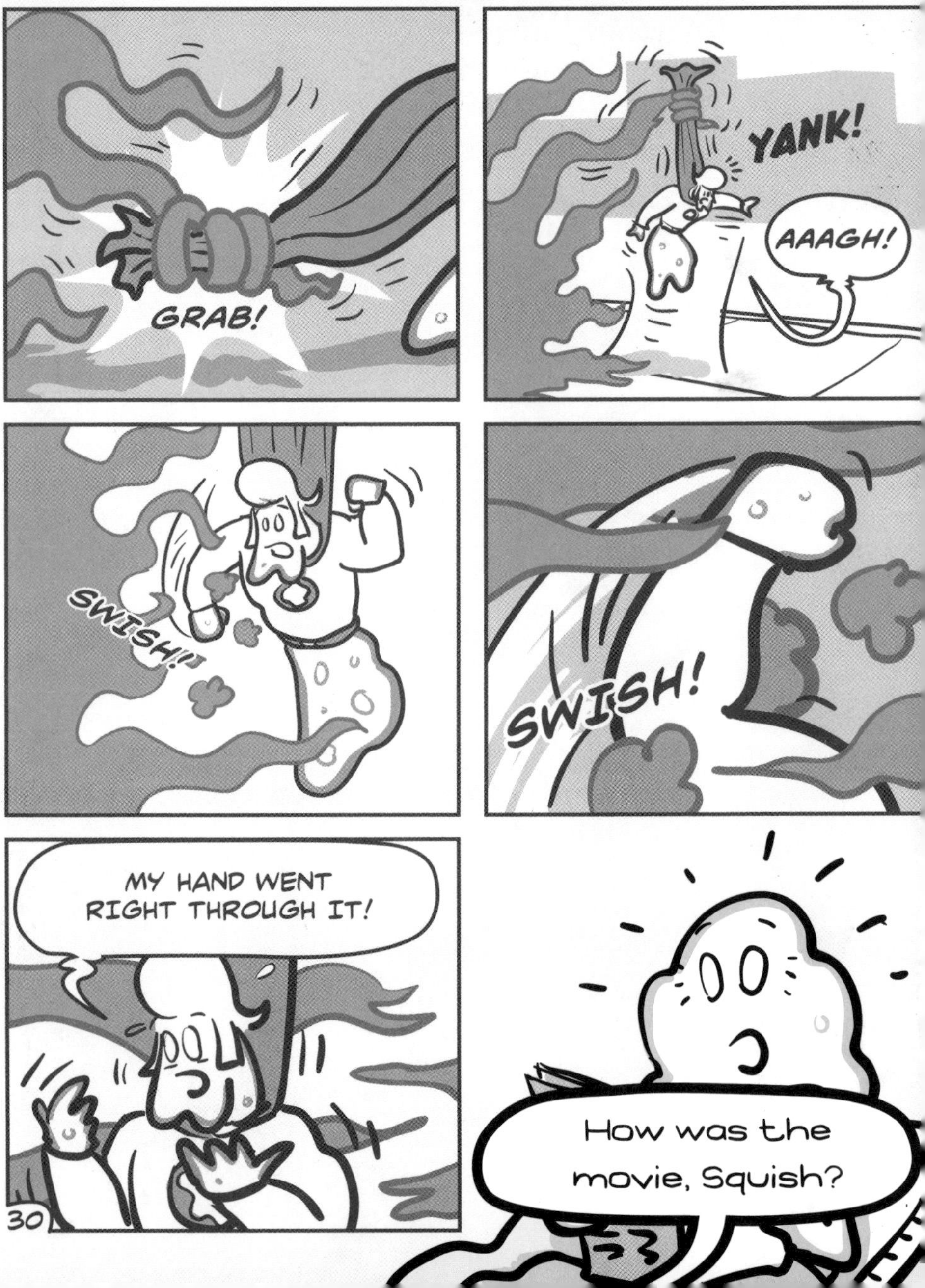
GRAB!
YANK!
AAAGH!
SWISH!!
SWISH!
MY HAND WENT RIGHT THROUGH IT!
How was the movie, Squish?

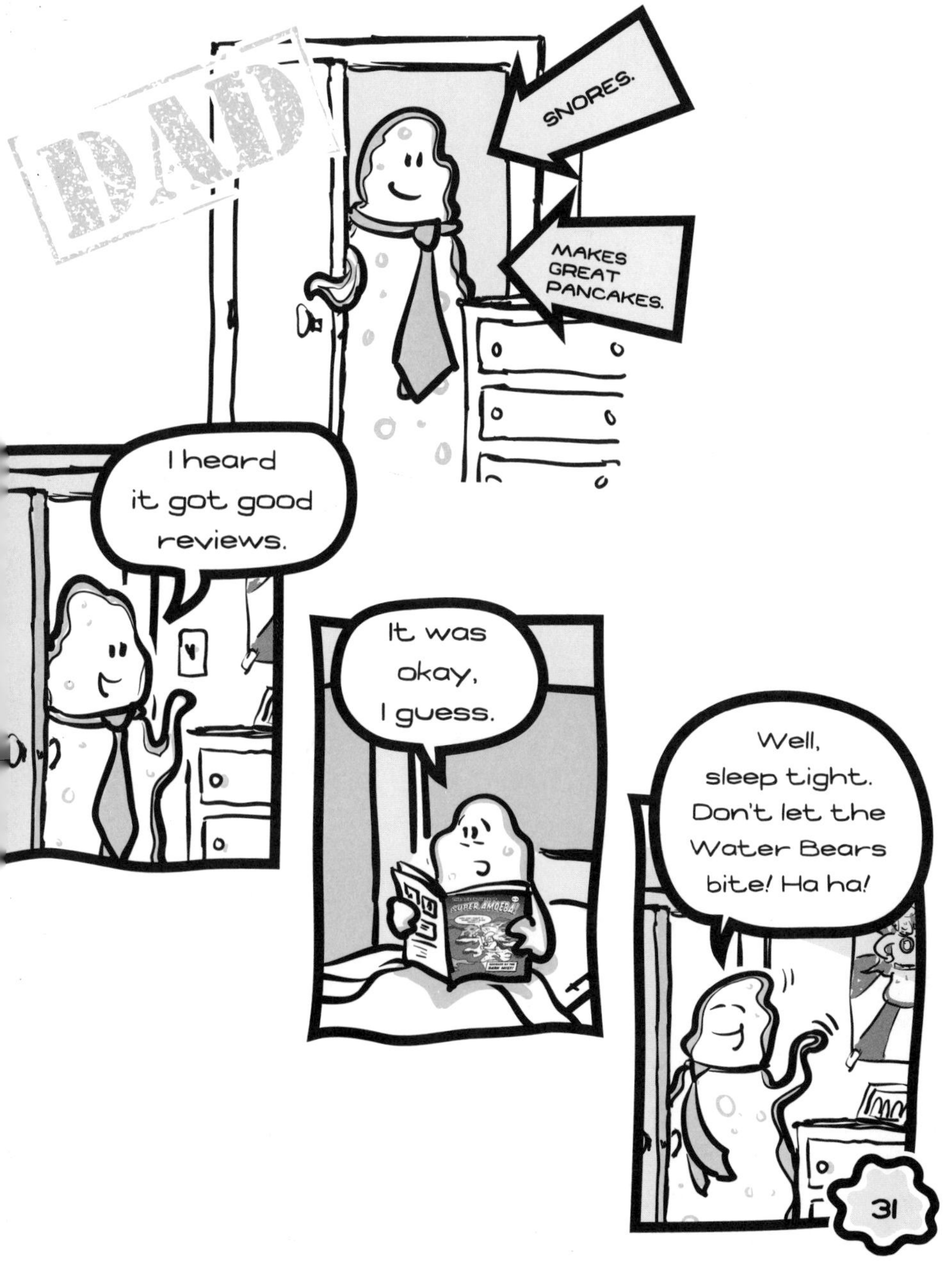
DAD
SNORES.
MAKES GREAT PANCAKES.
I heard it got good reviews.
It was okay, I guess.
SUPER AMOEBA!
Well, sleep tight. Don't let the Water Bears bite! Ha ha!

CLICK

Water Bears bite, yeah, heh-heh.

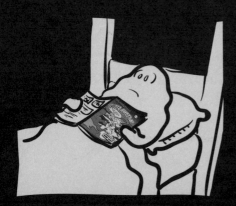

SCRAAAAATCH...

ZIP!

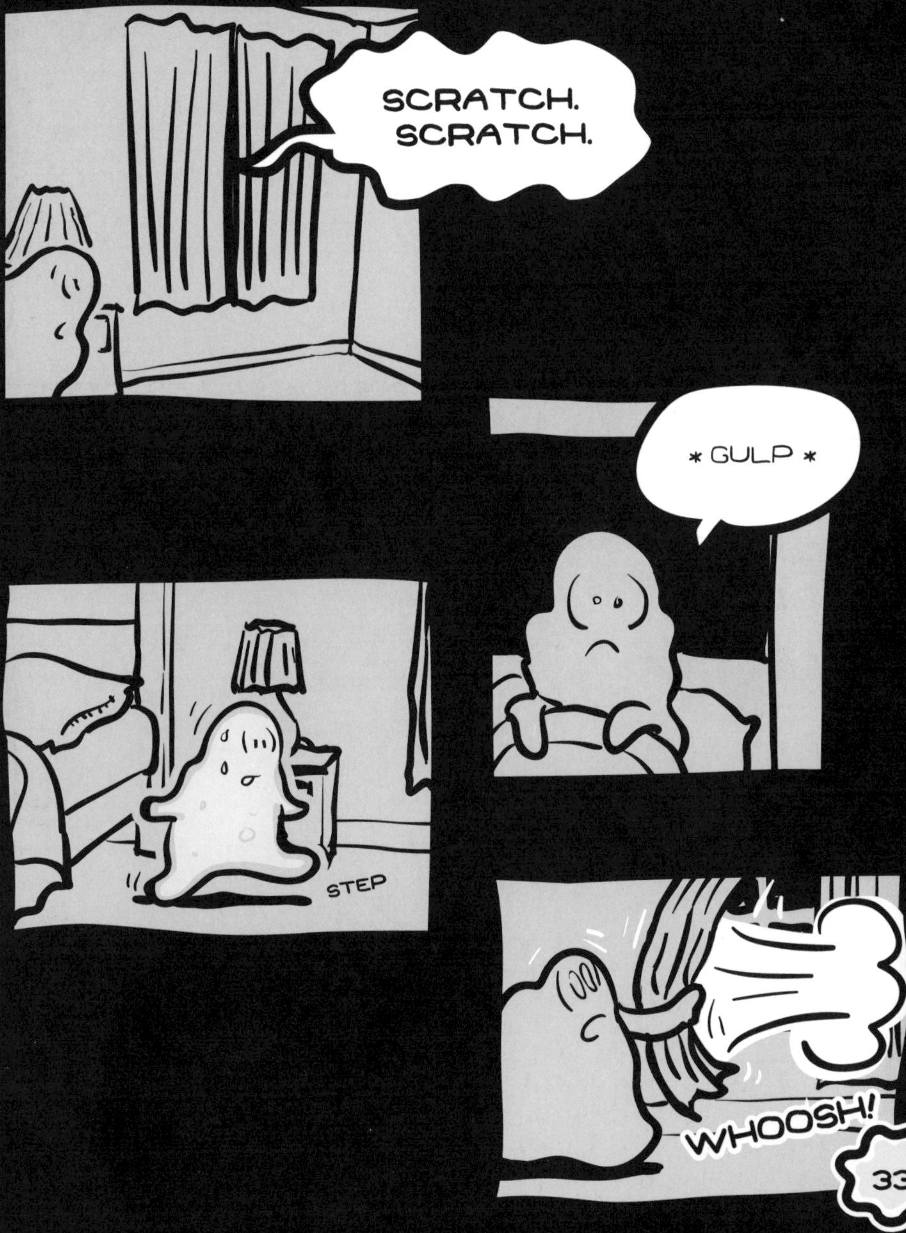
SCRATCH.
SCRATCH.
* GULP *
STEP
WHOOSH!

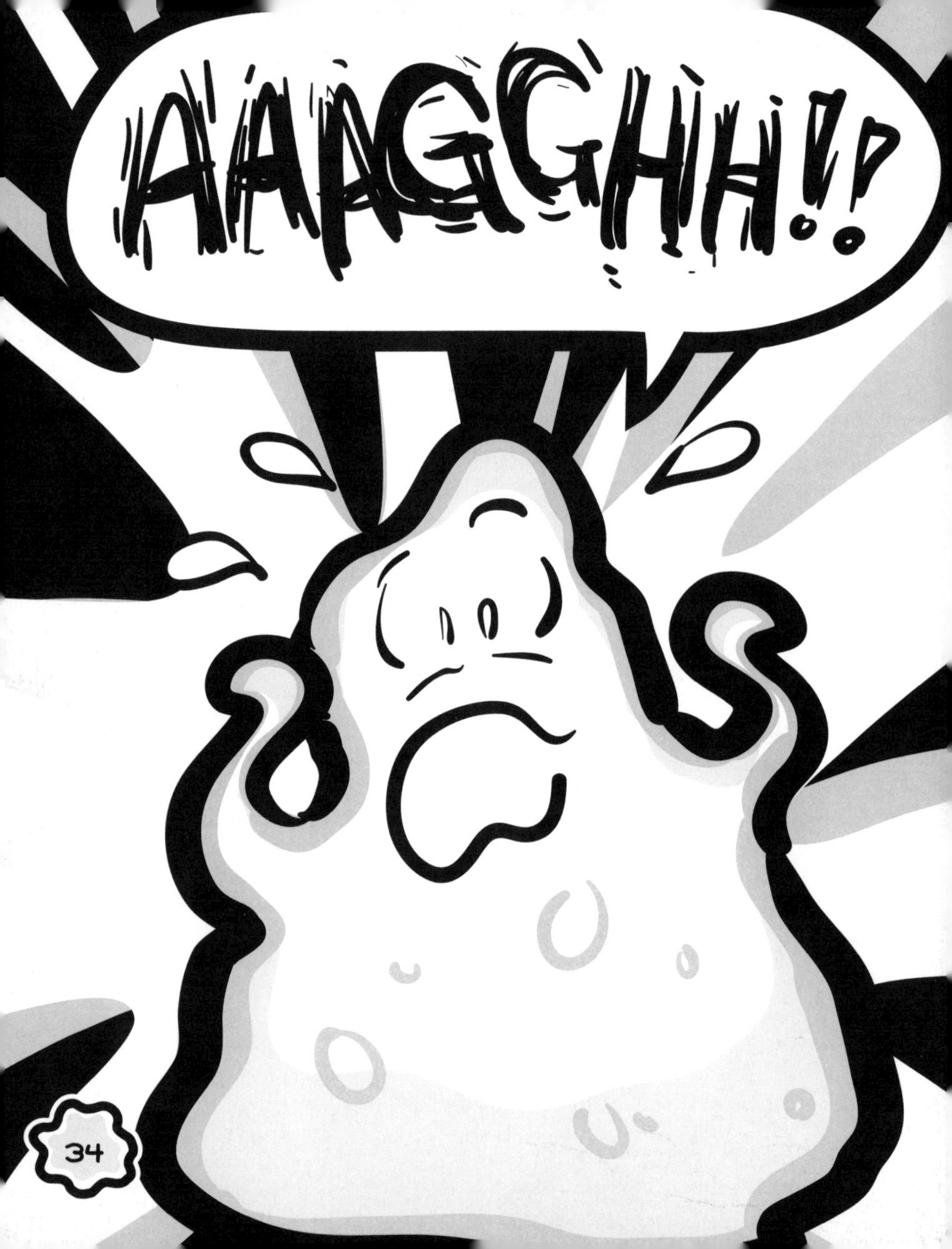
AAAGGHH!!

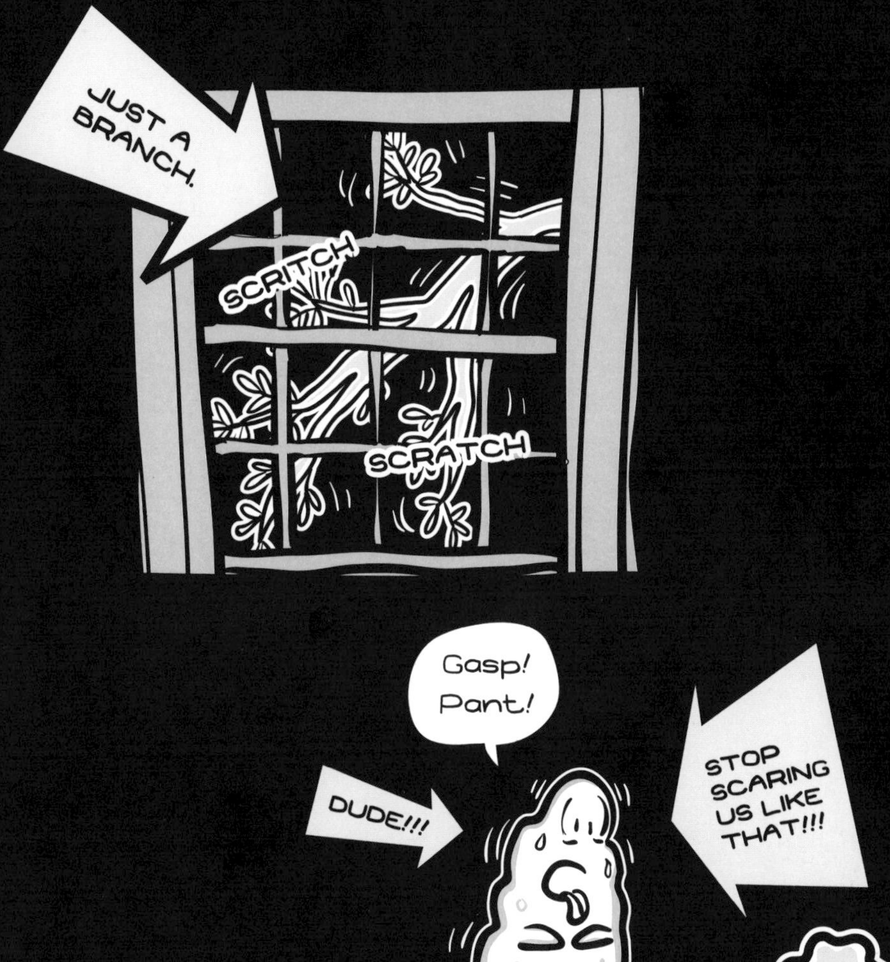
JUST A BRANCH.
SCRITCH
SCRATCH
Gasp! Pant!
DUDE!!!
STOP SCARING US LIKE THAT!!!

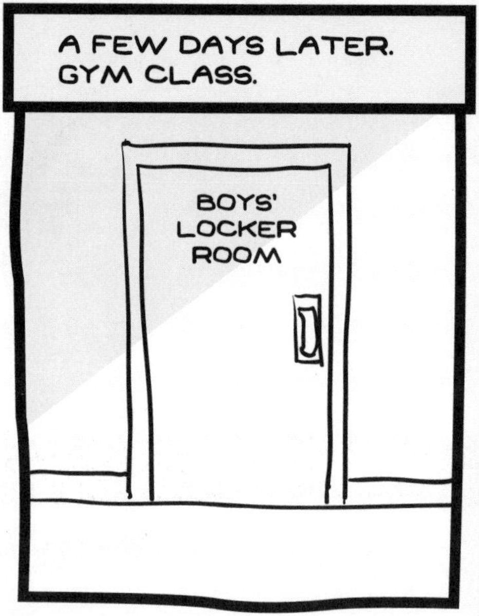
A FEW DAYS LATER.
GYM CLASS.
BOYS'
LOCKER
ROOM

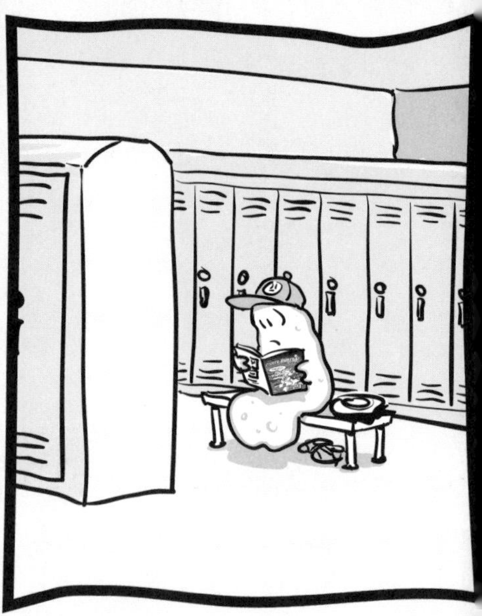

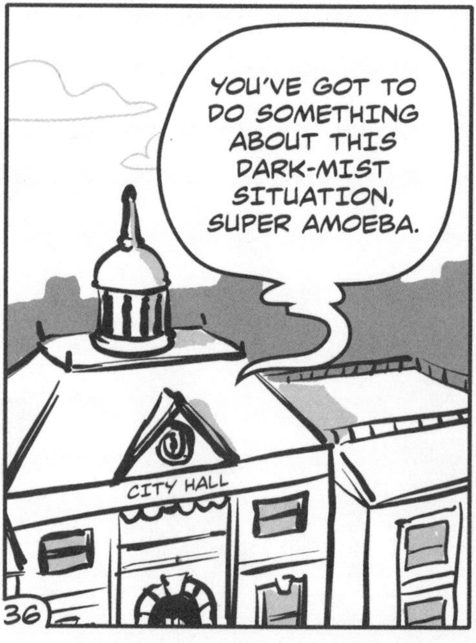
YOU'VE GOT TO DO SOMETHING ABOUT THIS DARK-MIST SITUATION, SUPER AMOEBA.
CITY HALL

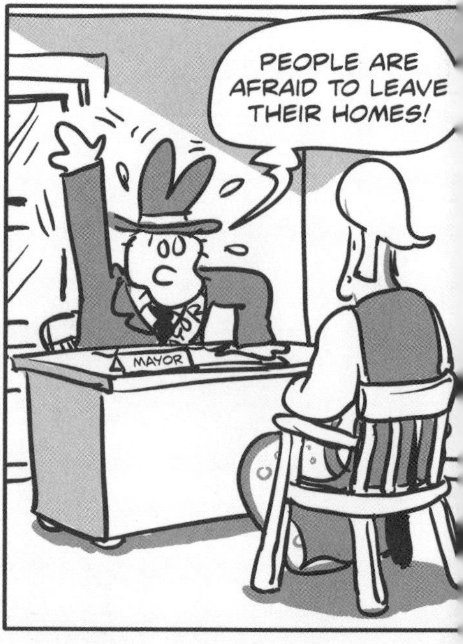
PEOPLE ARE AFRAID TO LEAVE THEIR HOMES!
MAYOR

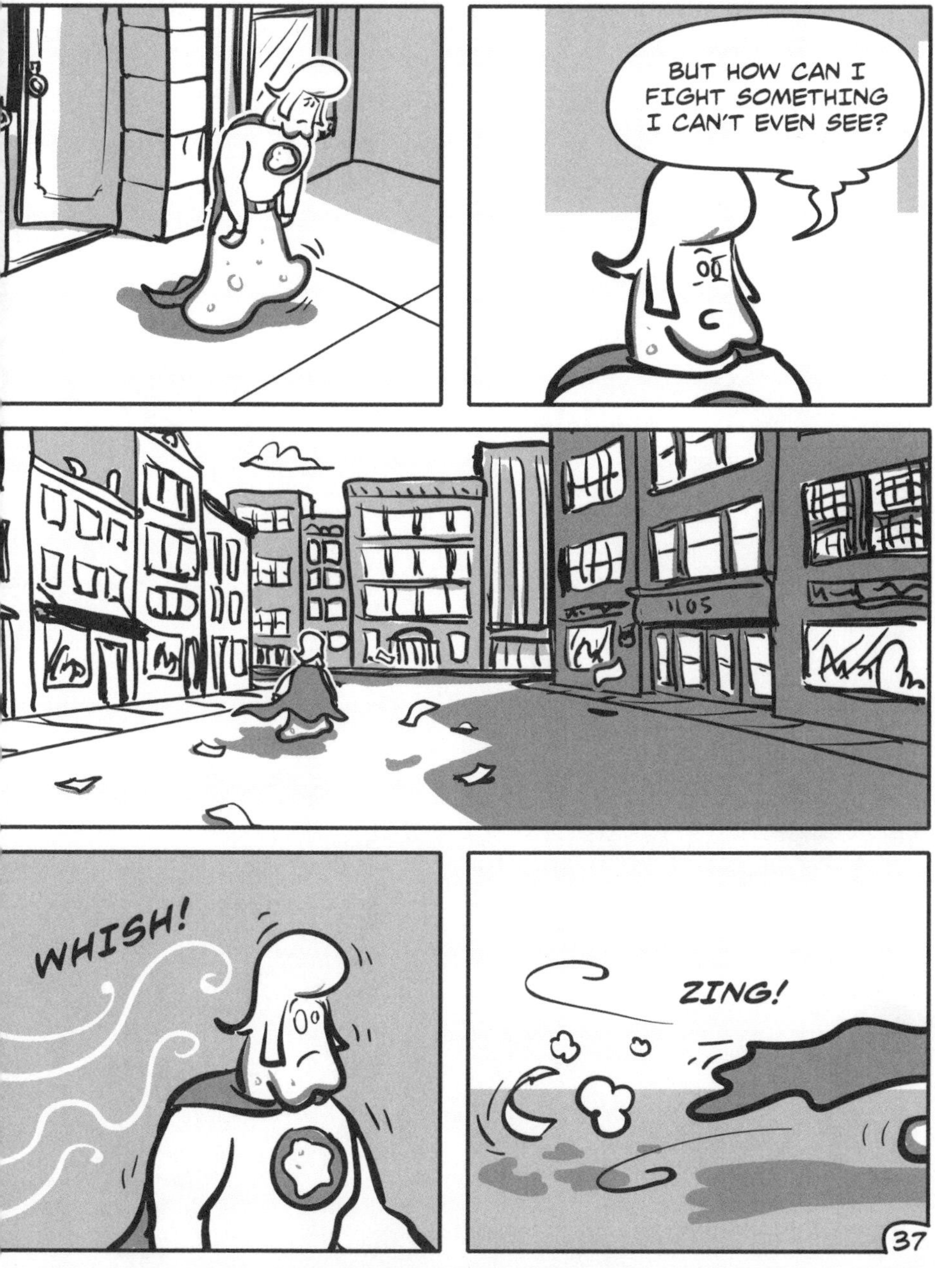
BUT HOW CAN I FIGHT SOMETHING I CAN'T EVEN SEE?
1105
WHISH!
ZING!

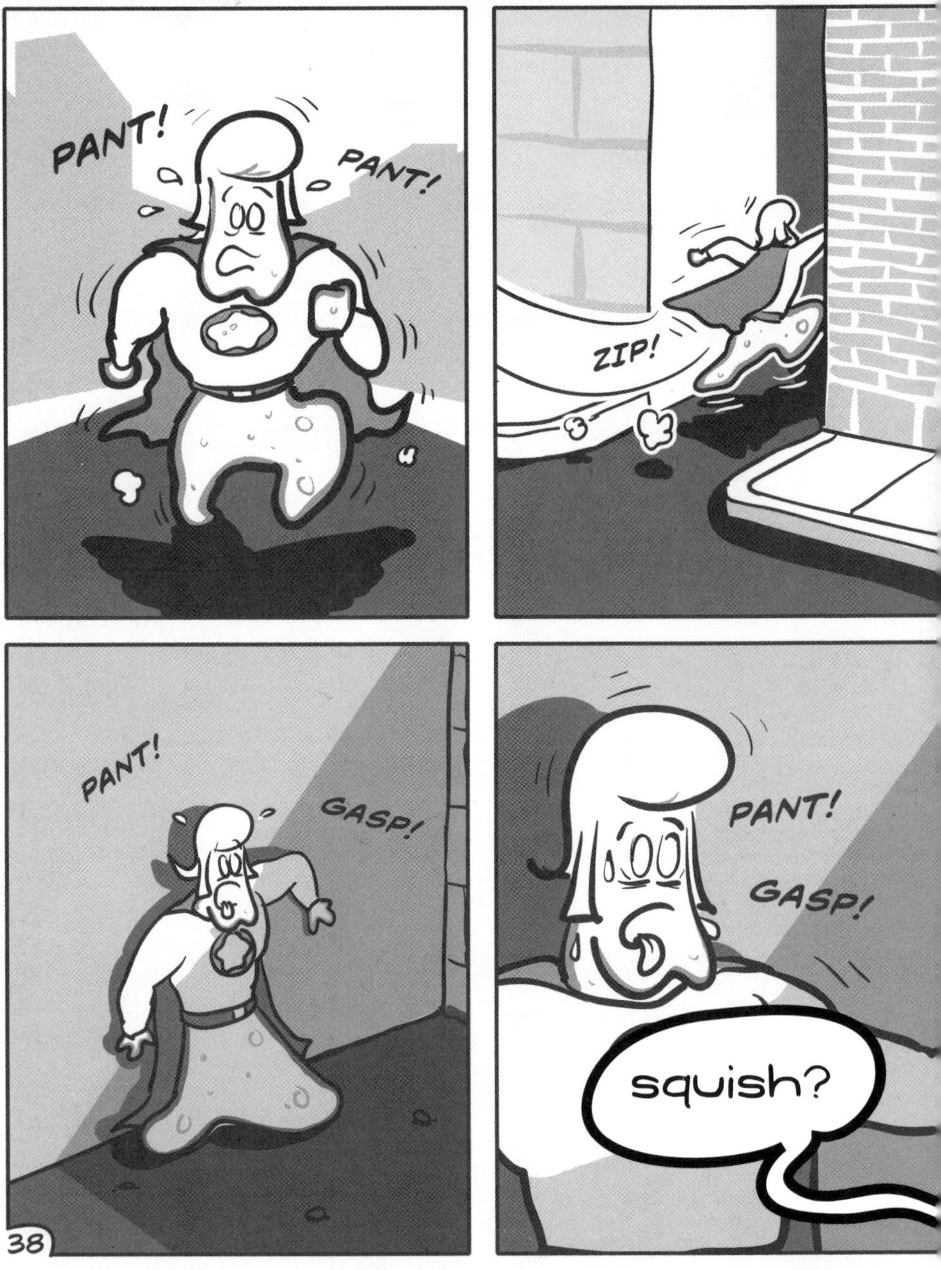
PANT!
PANT!
ZIP!
PANT!
GASP!
PANT!
GASP!
squish?

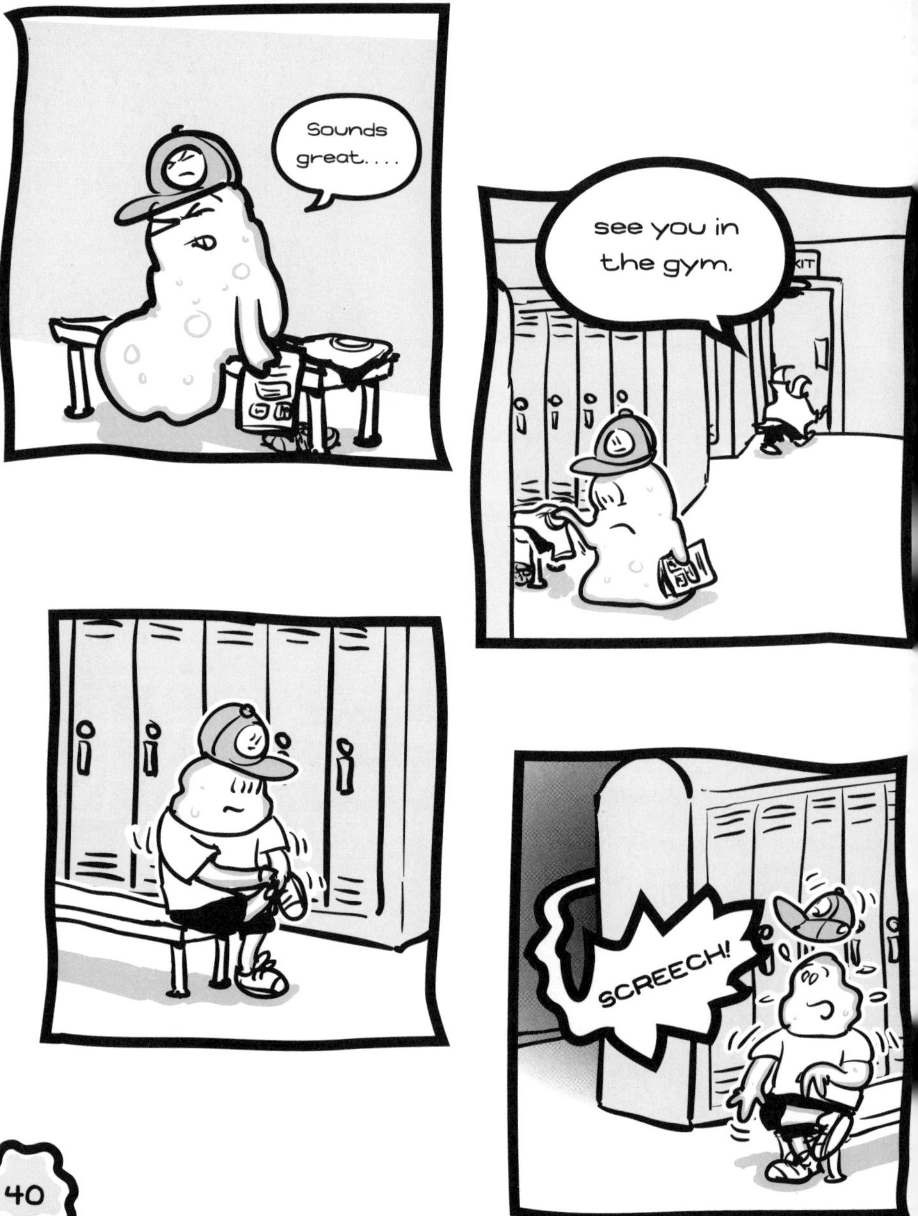
Sounds great. . . .
see you in the gym.
SCREECH!

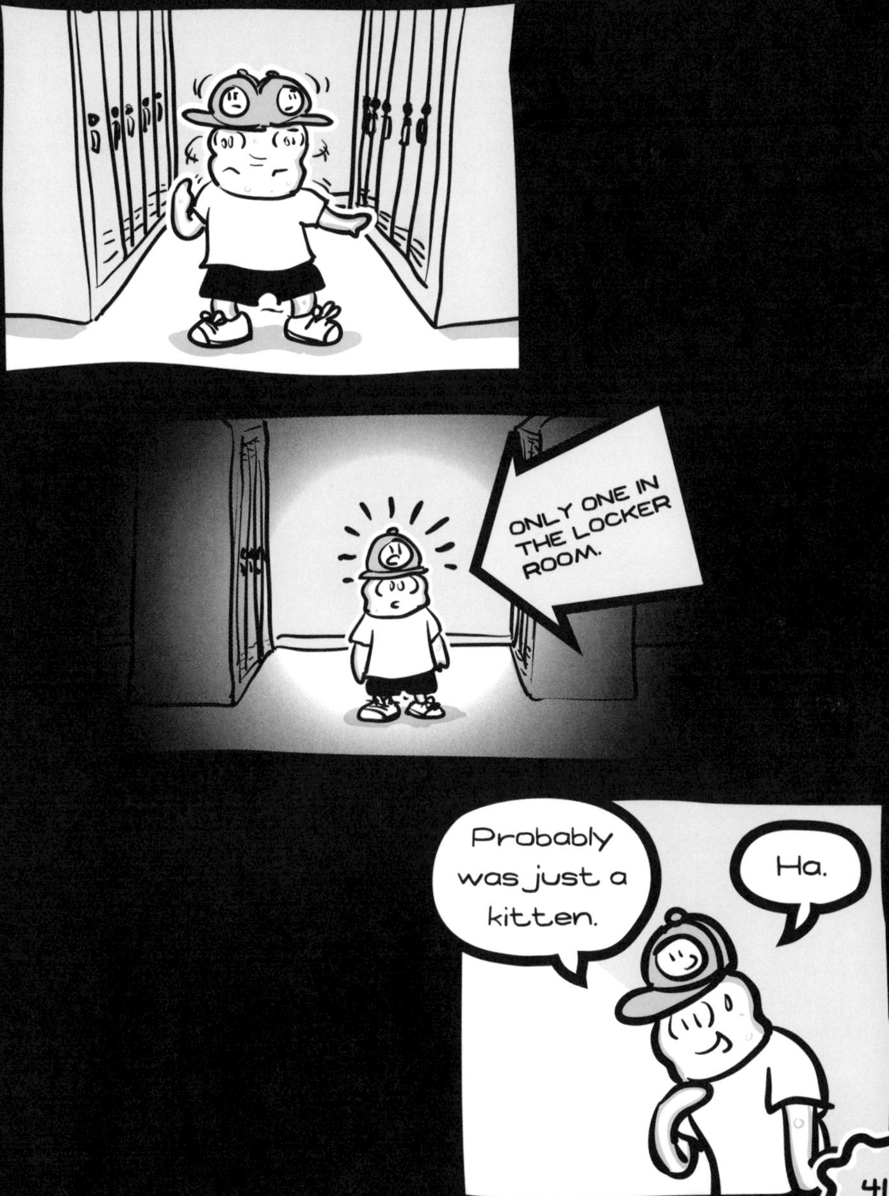
ONLY ONE IN THE LOCKER ROOM.
Probably was just a kitten.
Ha.

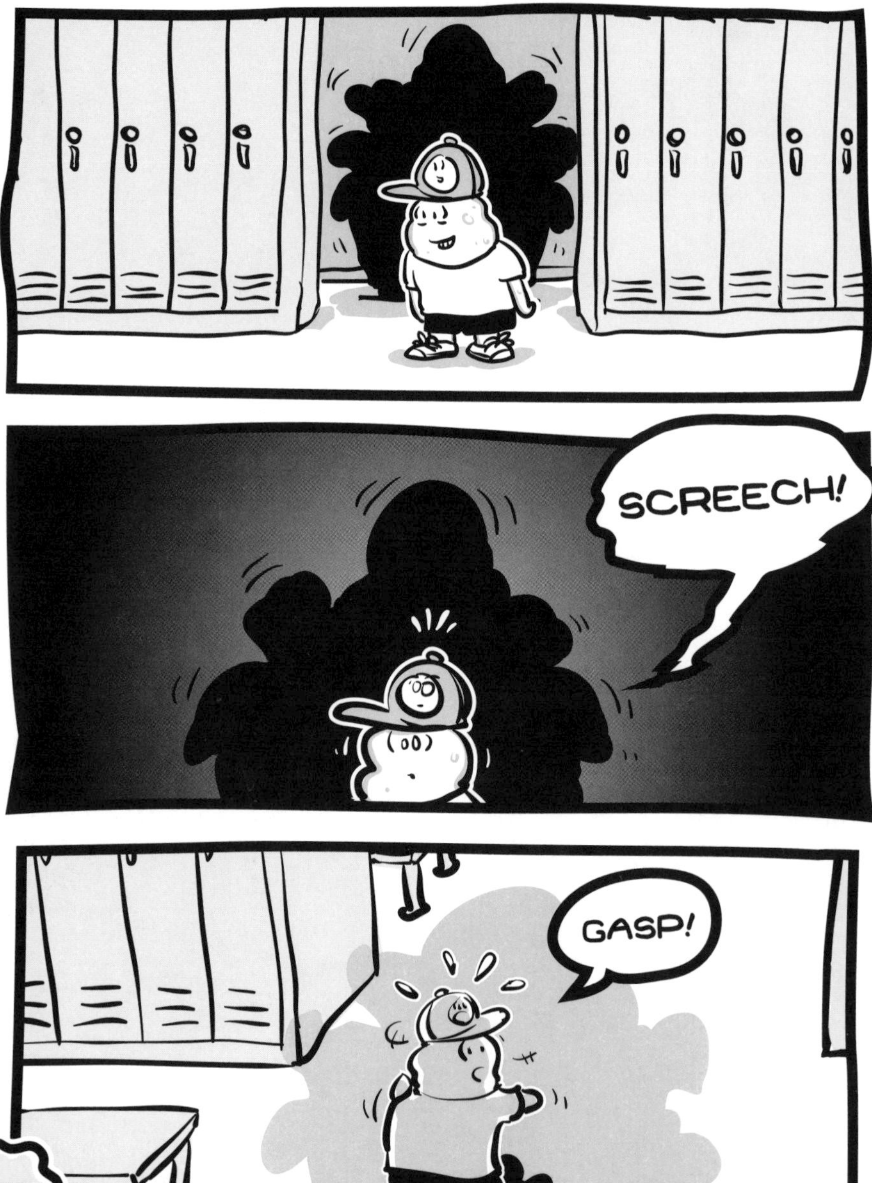
SCREECH!
GASP!

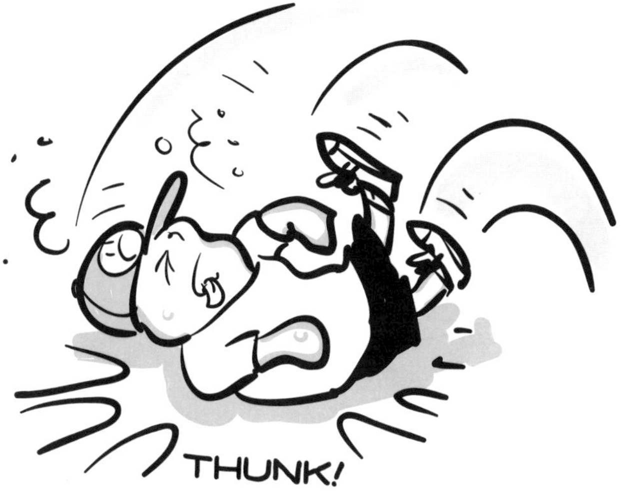
THUNK!

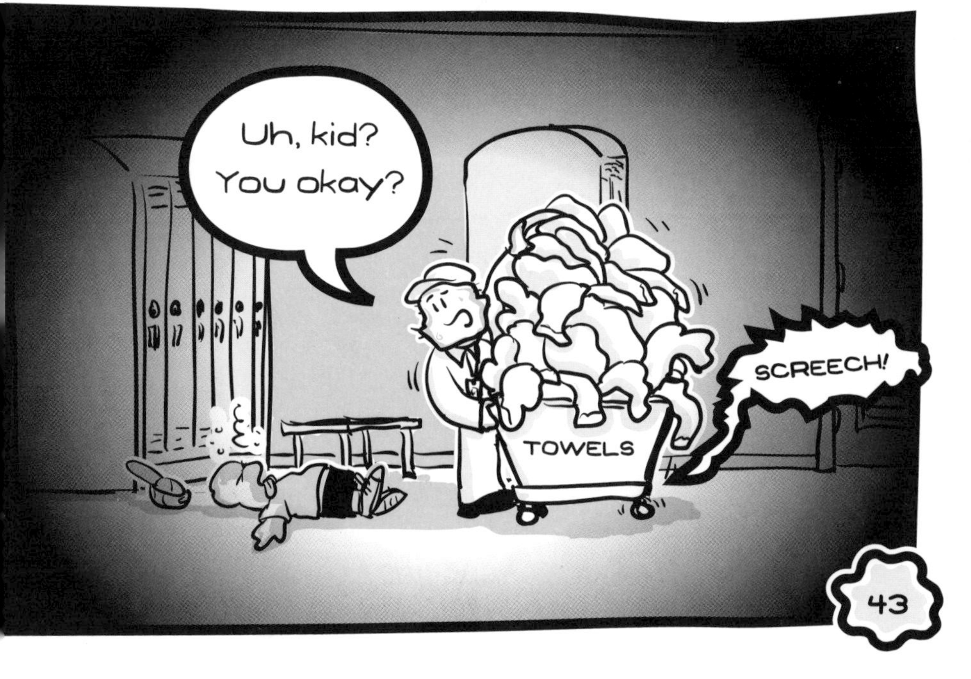
Uh, kid? You okay?
TOWELS
SCREECH!

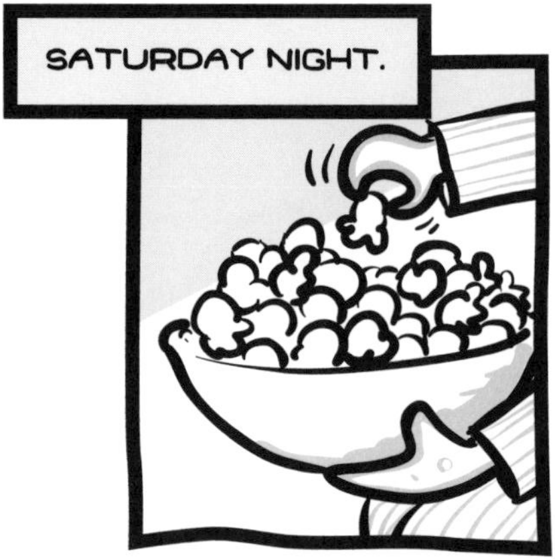
SATURDAY NIGHT.

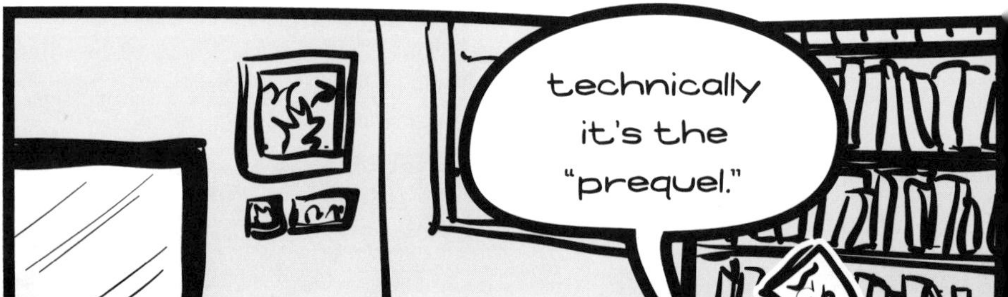
technically it's the "prequel."

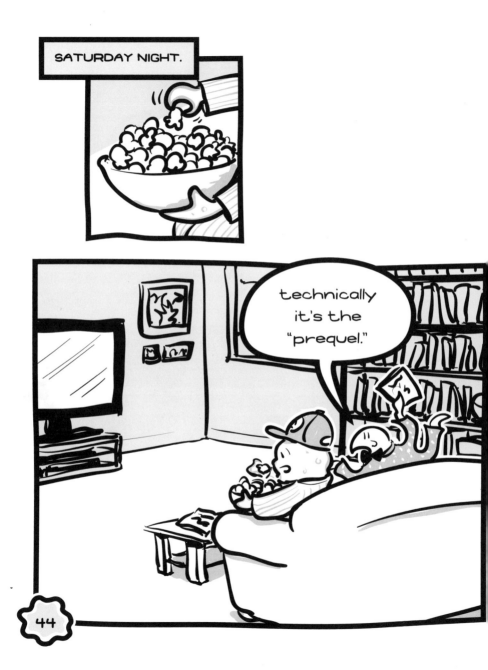

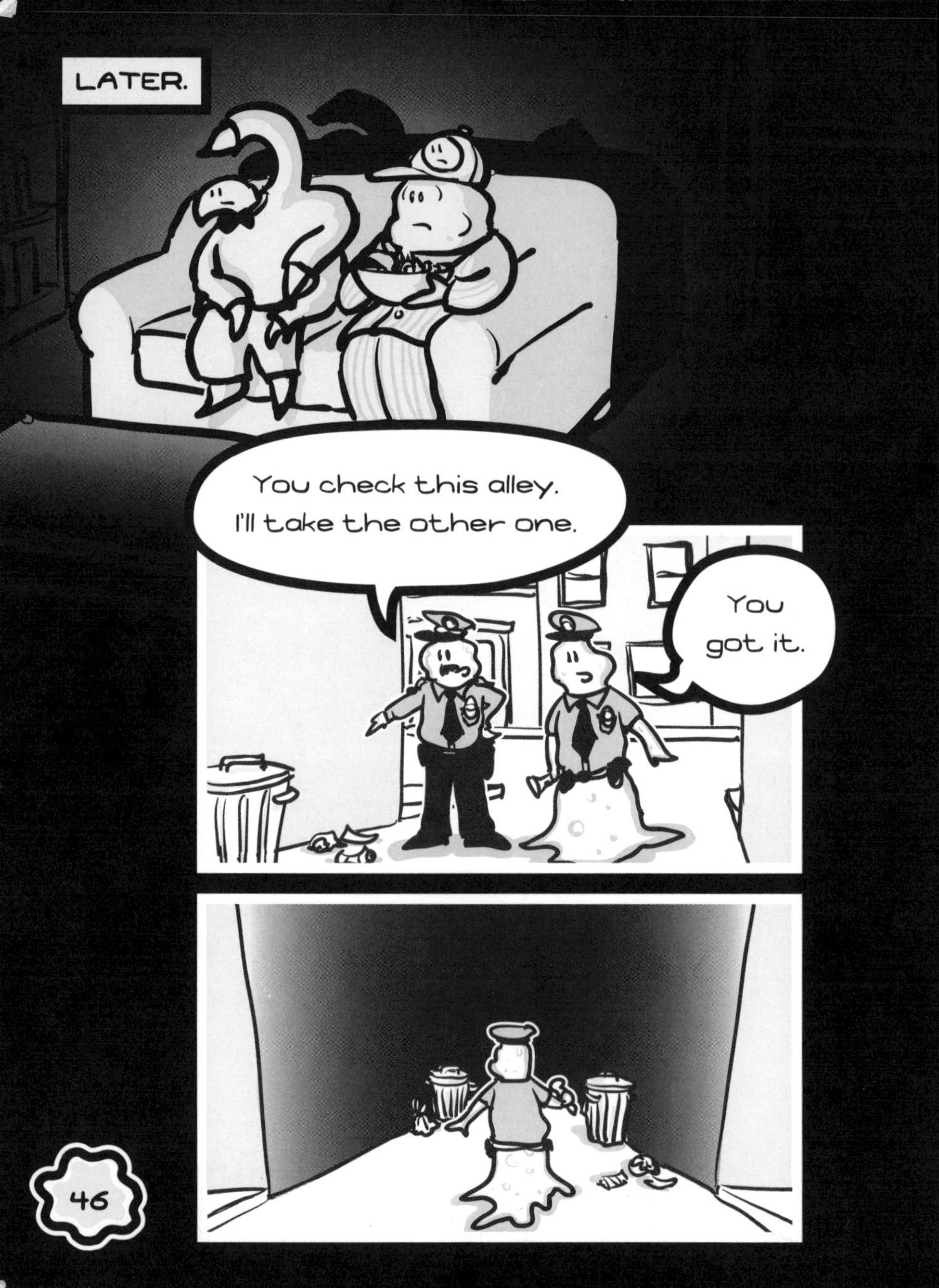
LATER.
You check this alley.
I'll take the other one.
You got it.

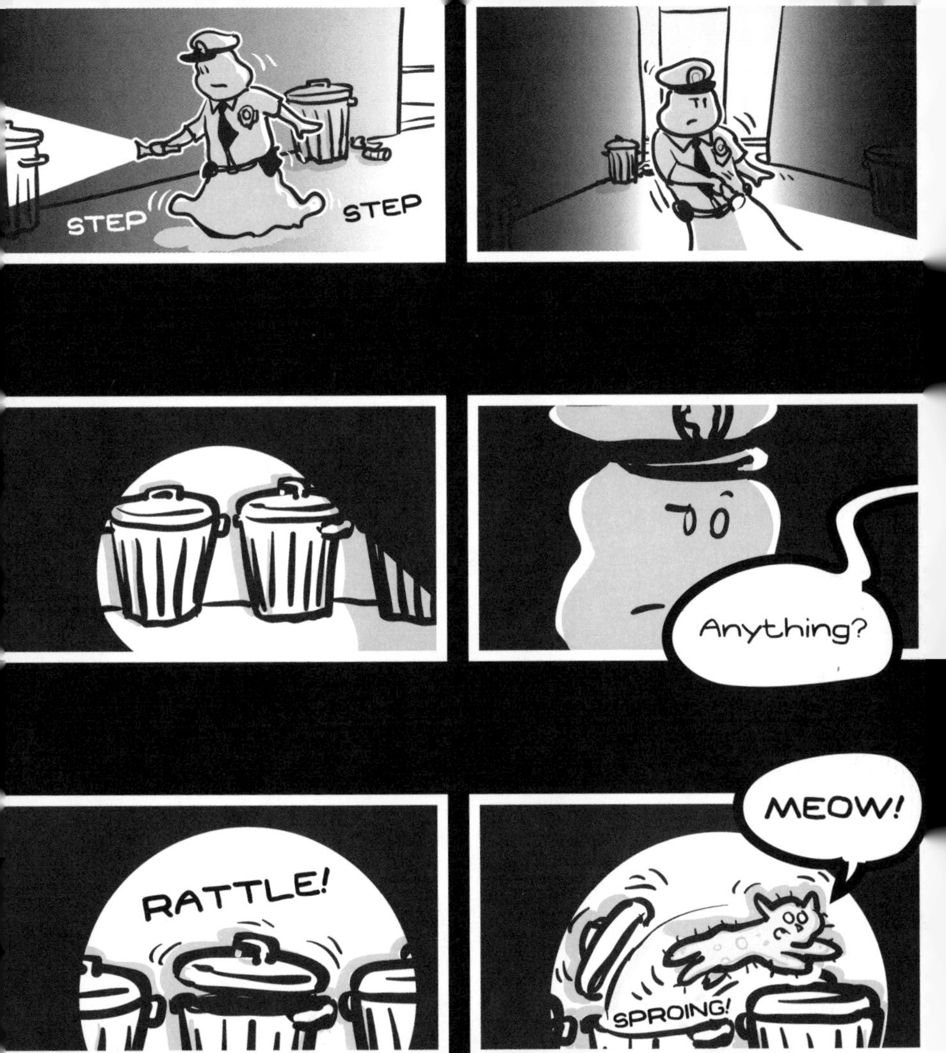
STEP
STEP
Anything?
RATTLE!
MEOW!
SPROING!

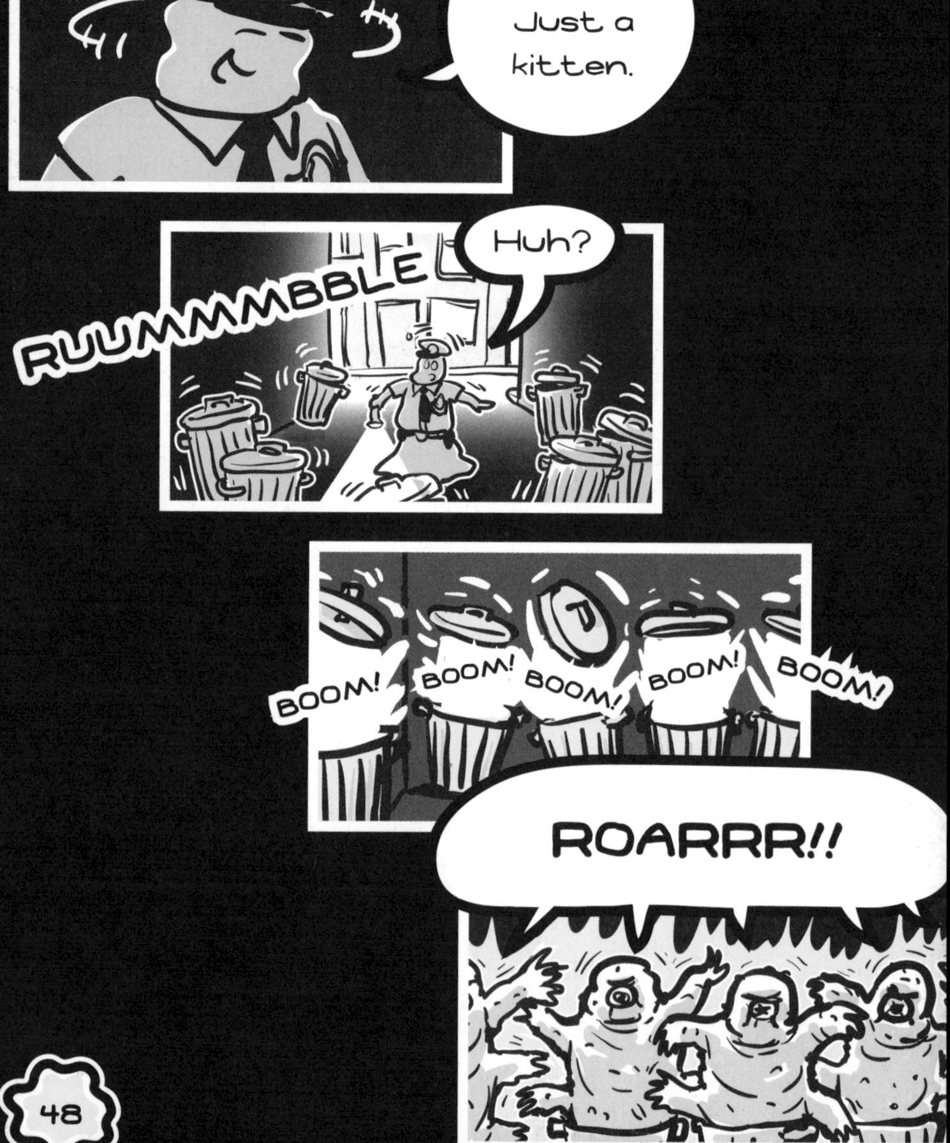
Just a kitten.
Huh?
RUUMMMMBBLE
BOOM!
BOOM!
BOOM!
BOOM!
BOOM!
ROARRR!!

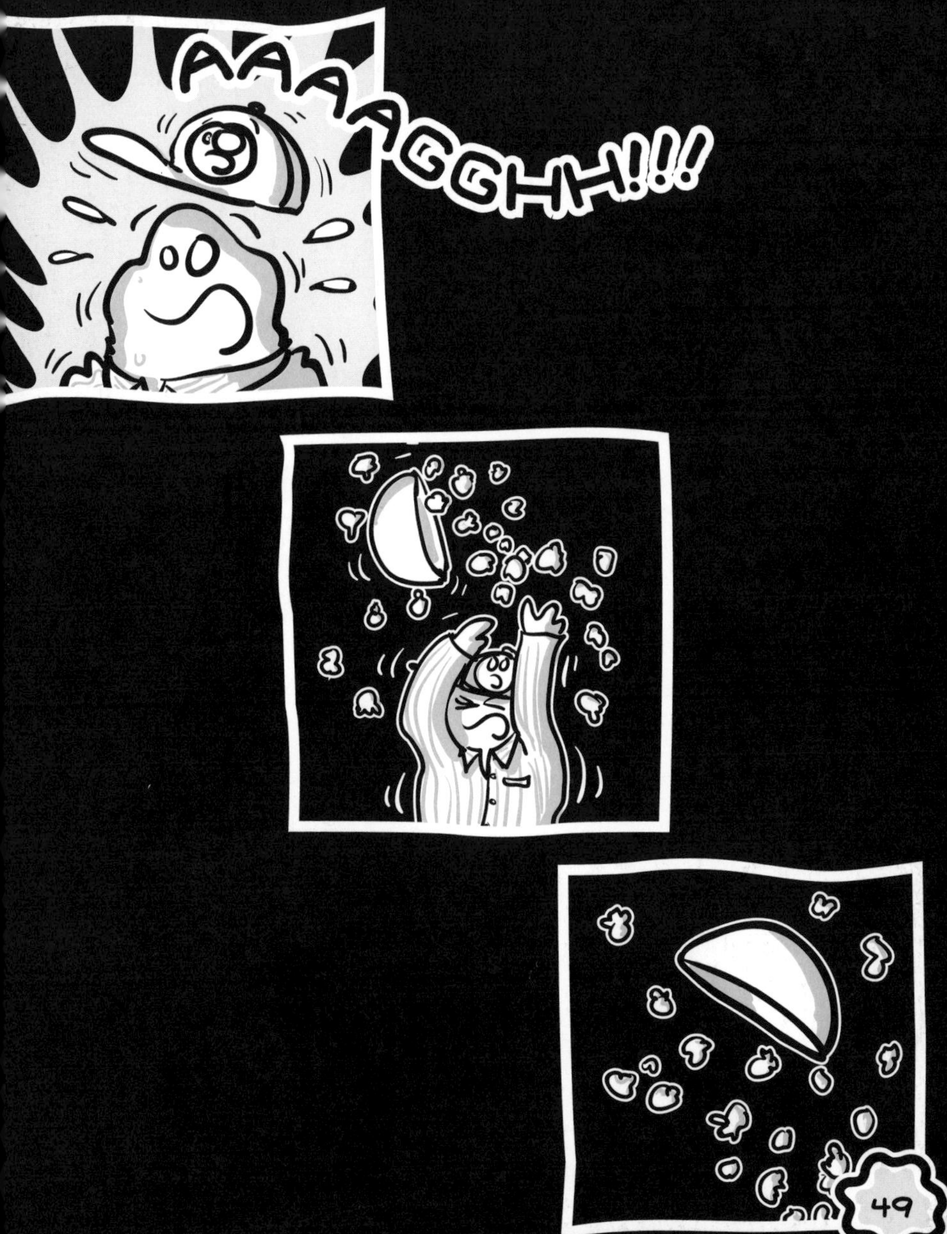
AAAAGGHH!!!

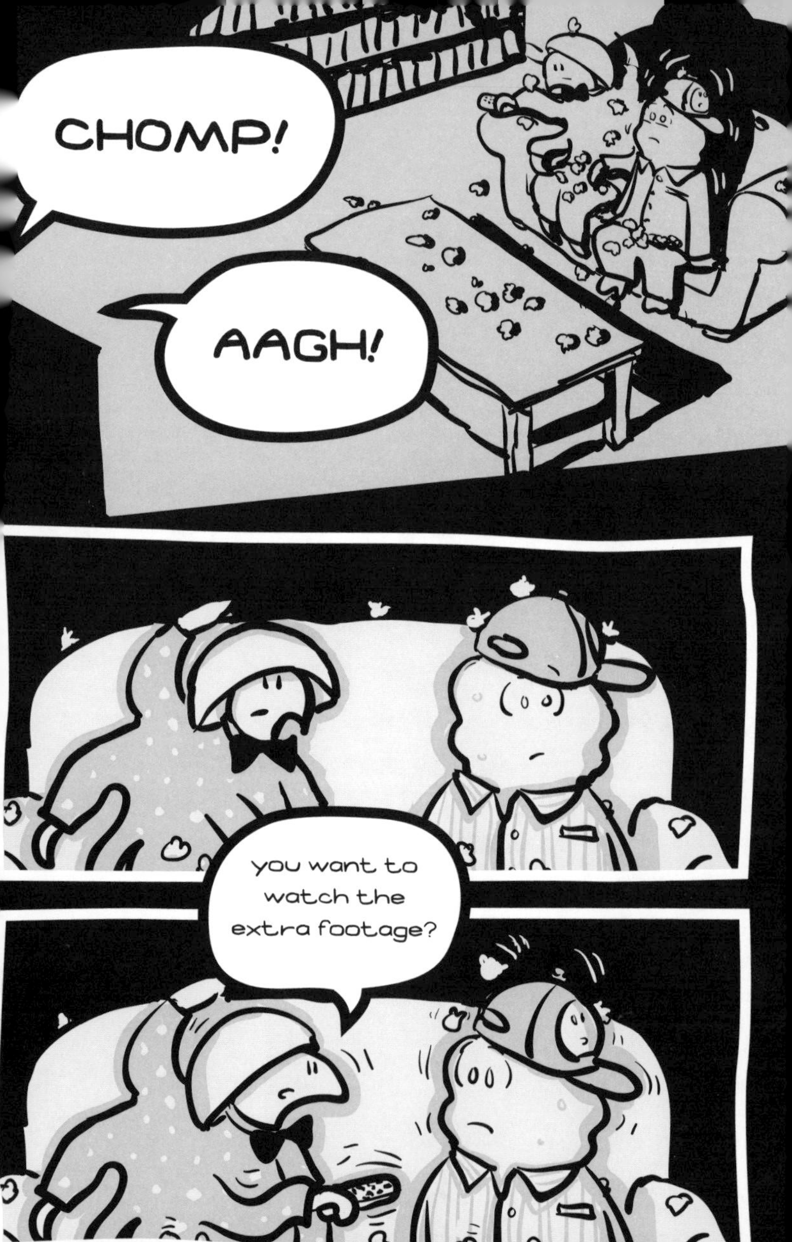
CHOMP!
AAGH!
you want to watch the extra footage?

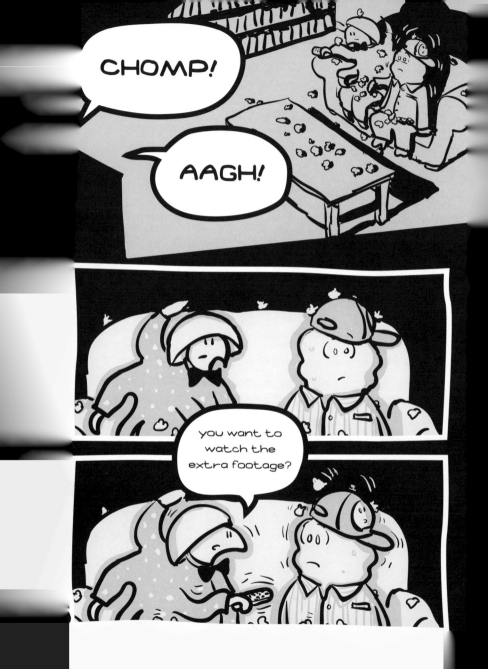

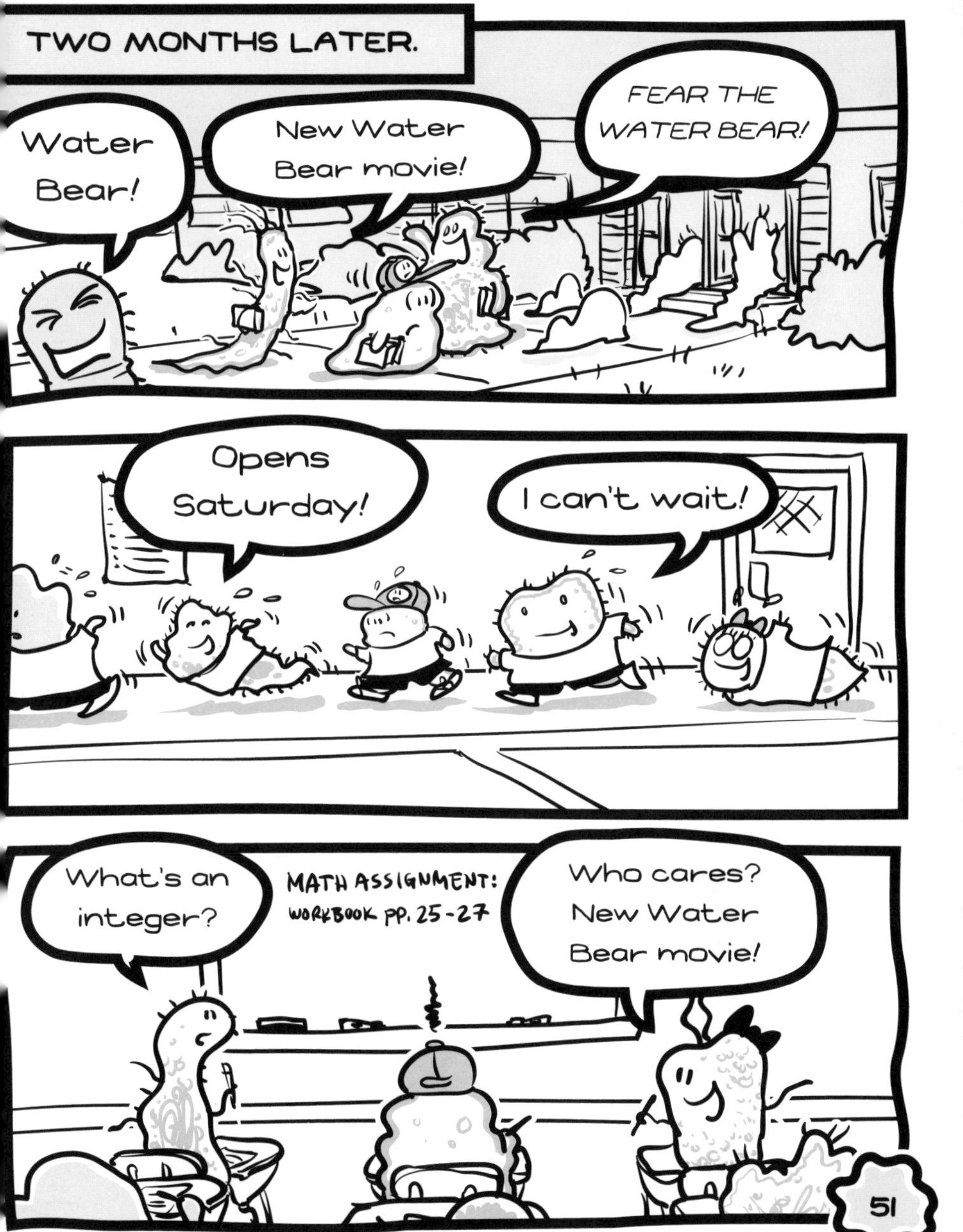
TWO MONTHS LATER.
Water Bear!
New Water Bear movie!
FEAR THE WATER BEAR!
Opens Saturday!
I can't wait!
What's an integer?
MATH ASSIGNMENT: WORKBOOK PP. 25-27
Who cares? New Water Bear movie!

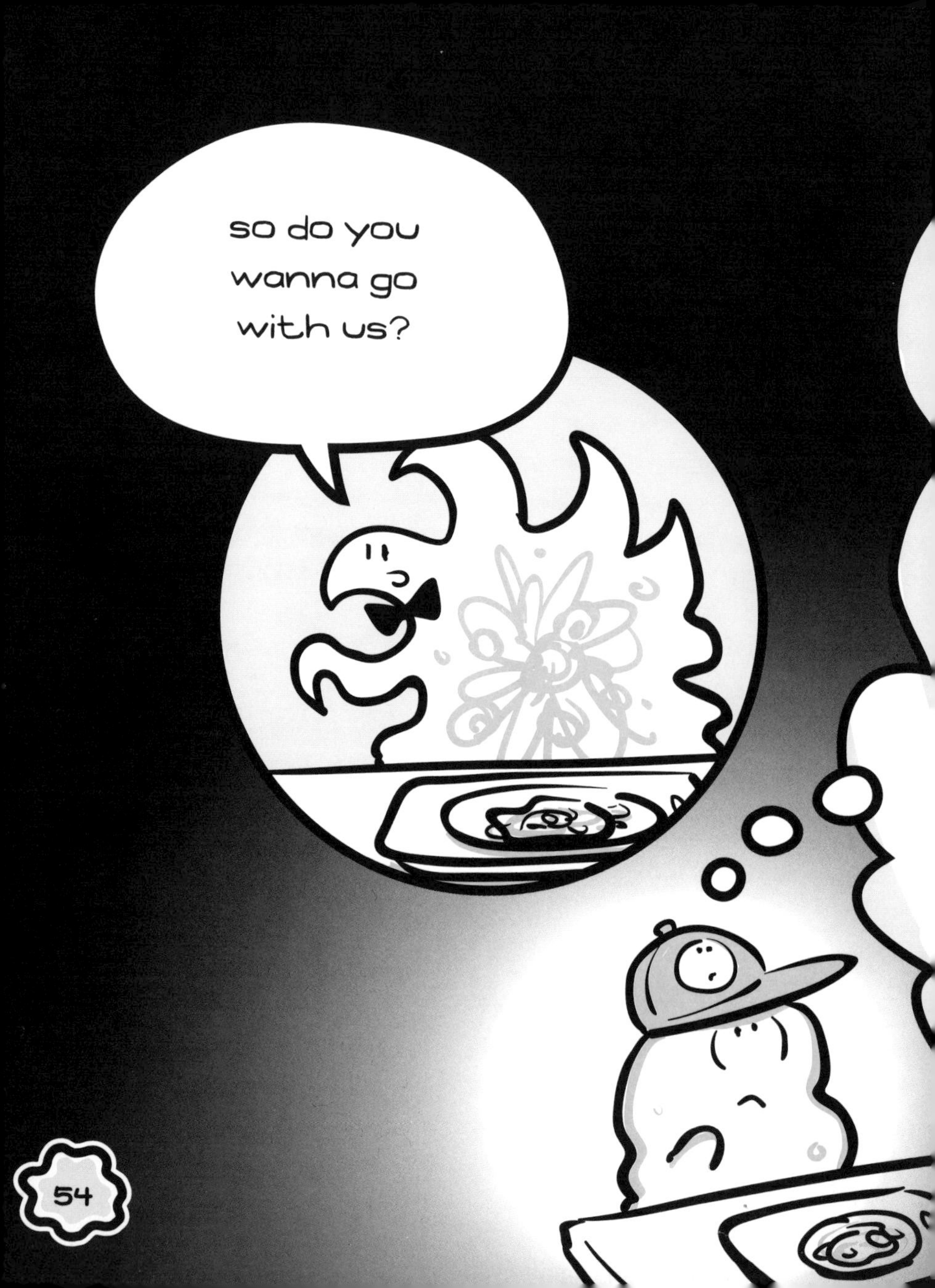
so do you wanna go with us?

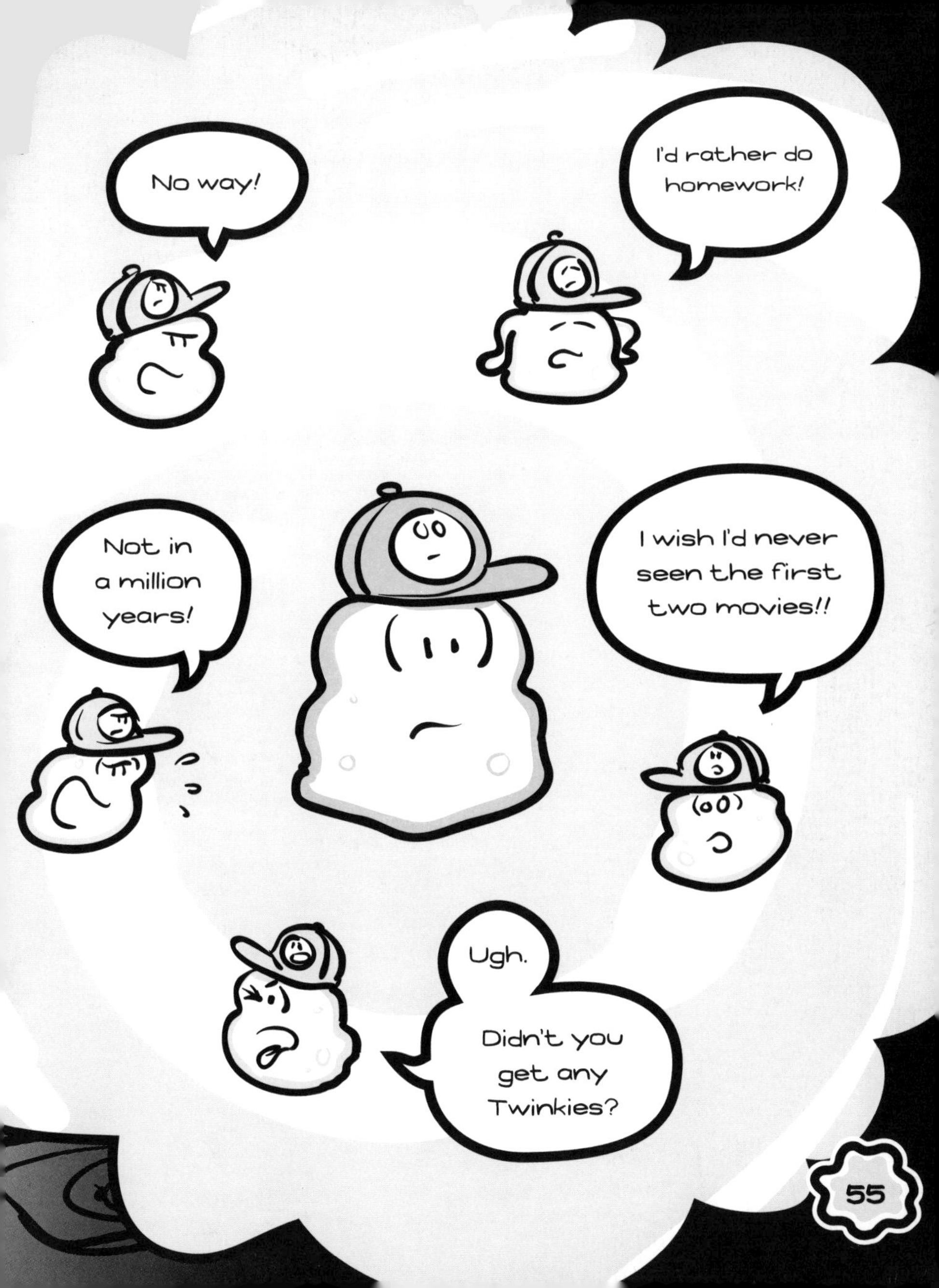
No way!
I'd rather do homework!
Not in a million years!
I wish I'd never seen the first two movies!!
Ugh.
Didn't you get any Twinkies?

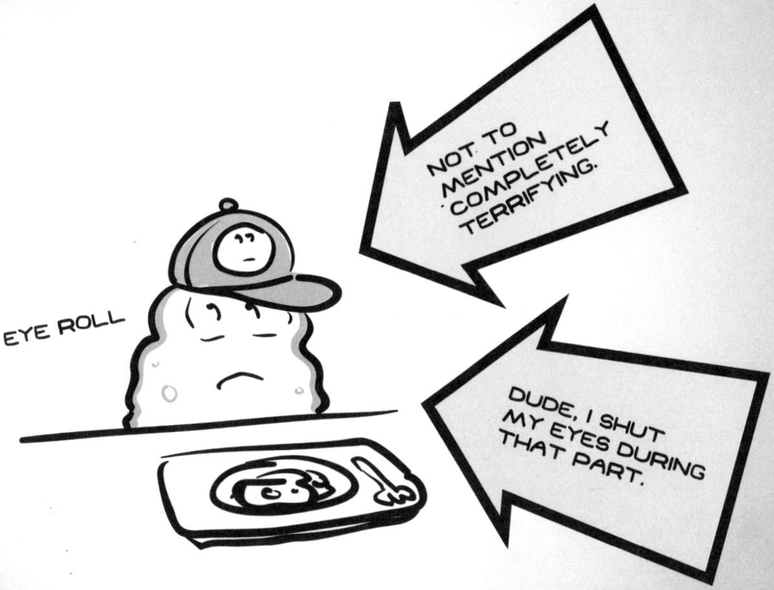
NOT TO MENTION COMPLETELY TERRIFYING.
EYE ROLL
DUDE, I SHUT MY EYES DURING THAT PART.

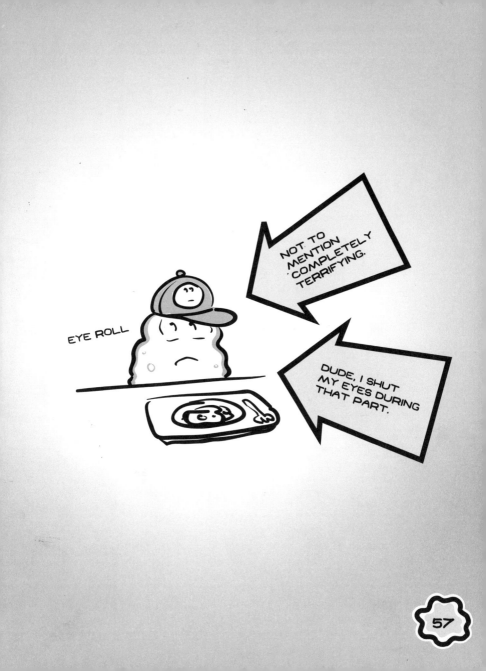

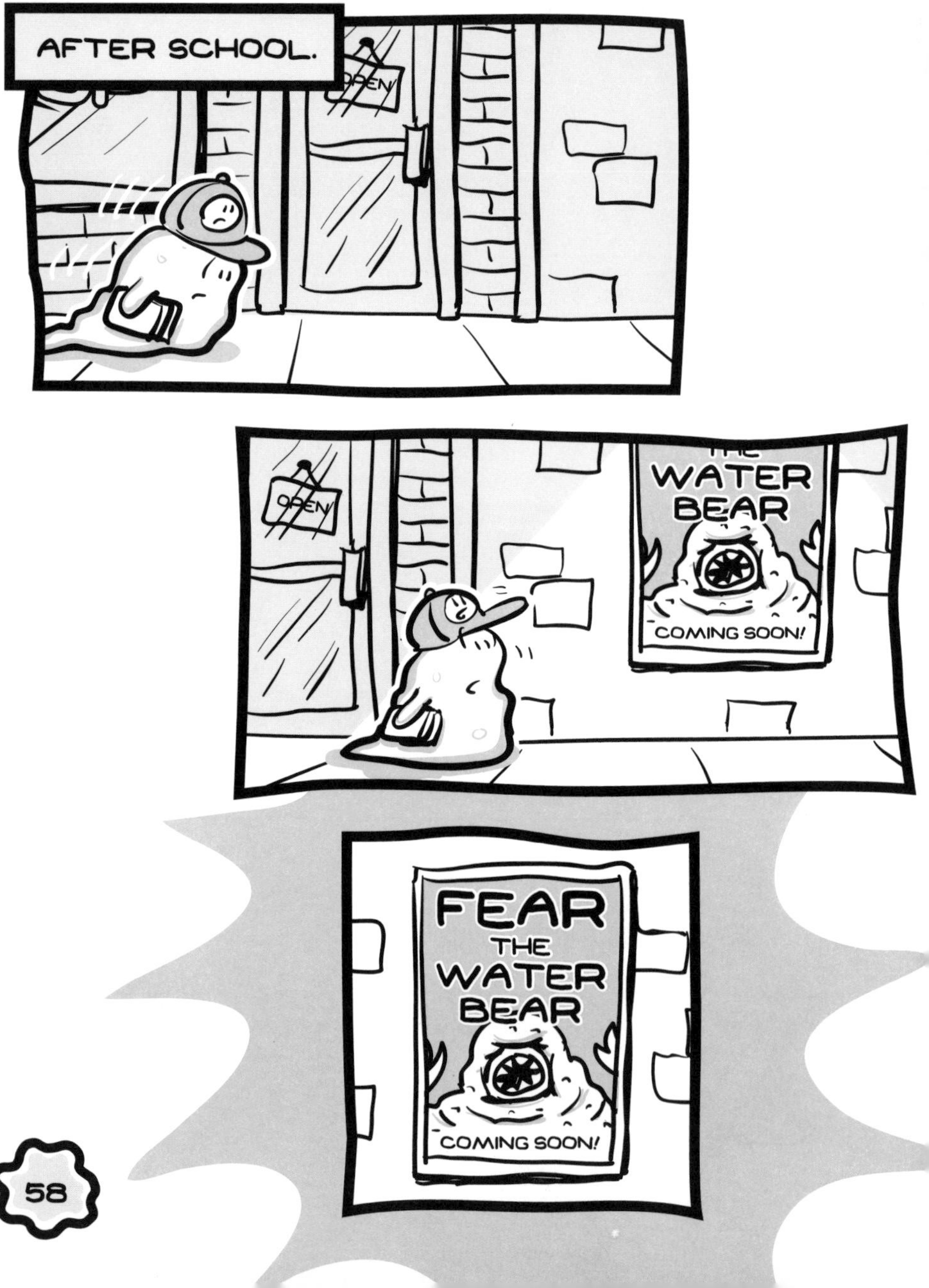
AFTER SCHOOL.
OPEN
OPEN
THE WATER BEAR
COMING SOON!
FEAR THE WATER BEAR
COMING SOON!

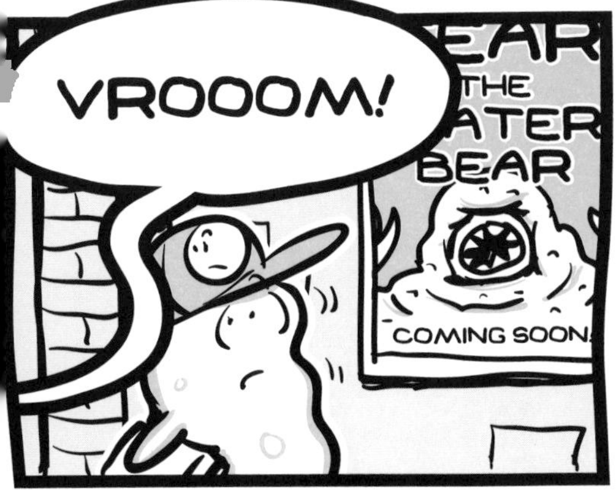
VROOOM!
EAR
THE
ATER
BEAR
COMING SOON

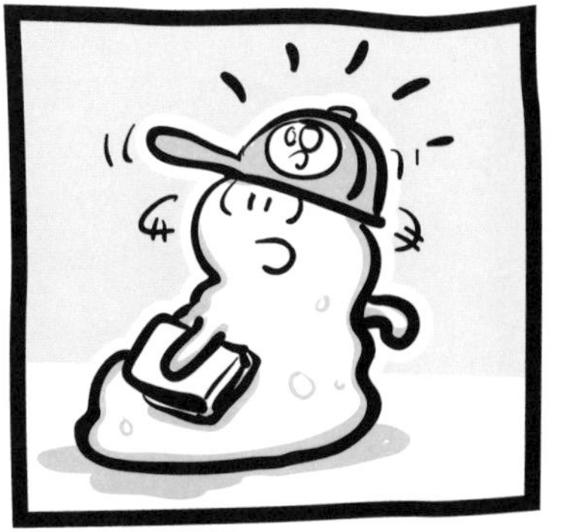

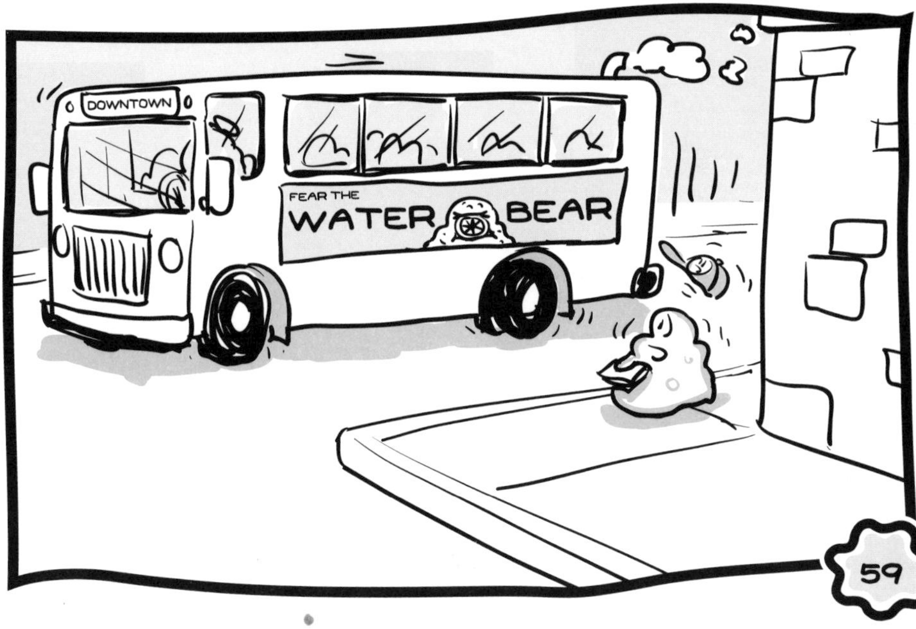
DOWNTOWN
FEAR THE
WATER BEAR

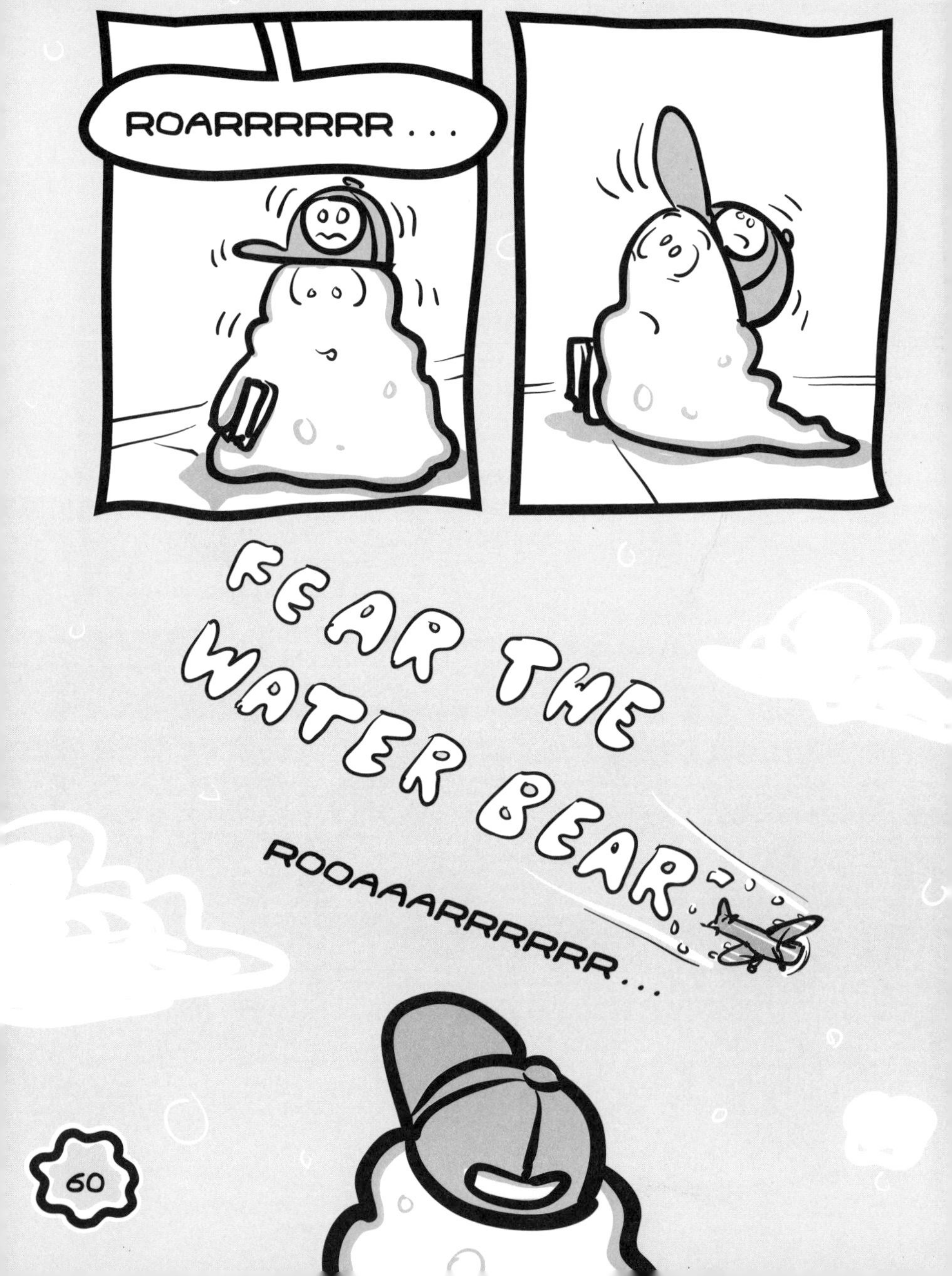
ROARRRRRR . . .
FEAR THE WATER BEAR
ROOAAAARRRRRRR . . .

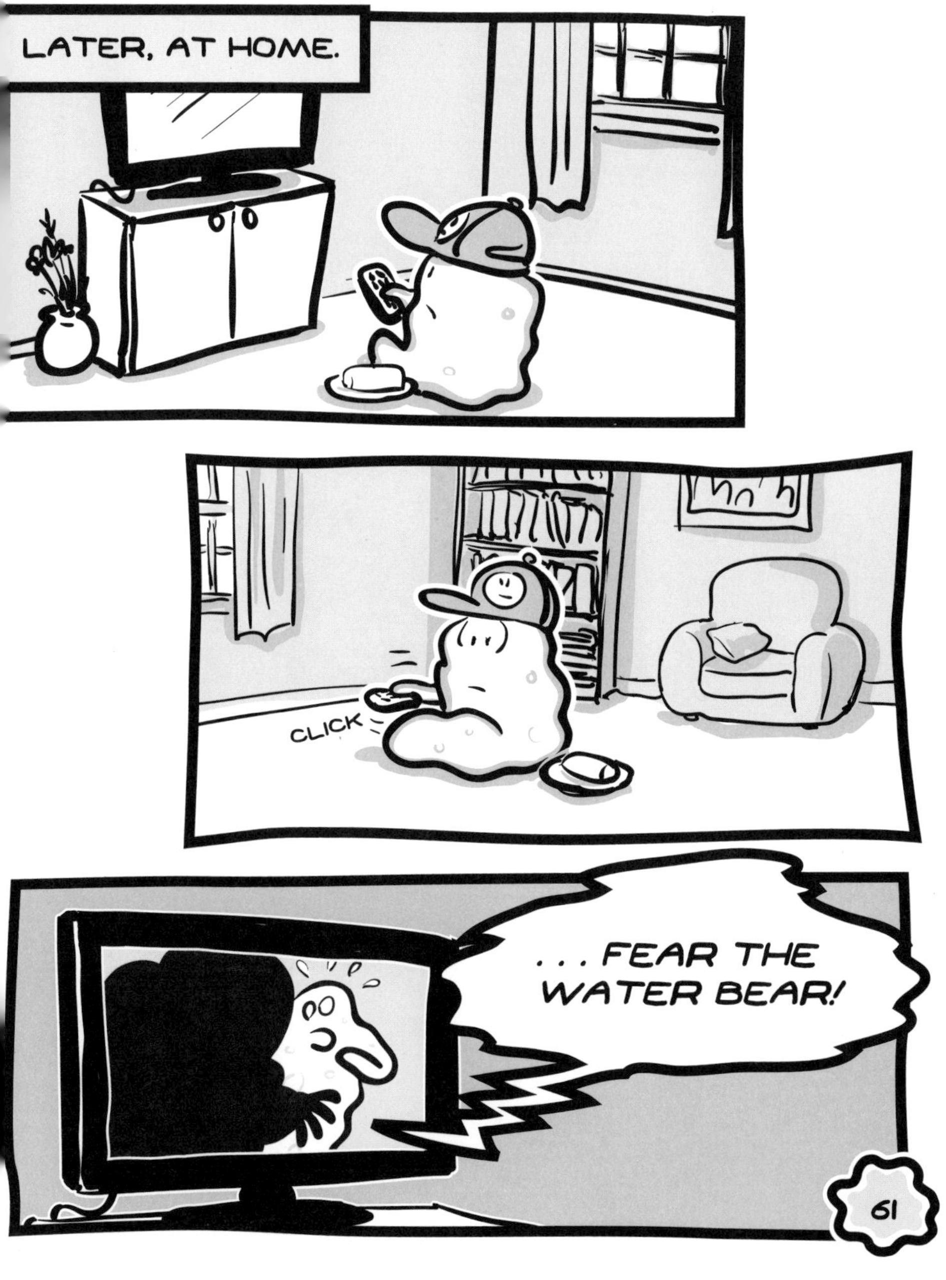
LATER, AT HOME.
CLICK
. . . FEAR THE WATER BEAR!

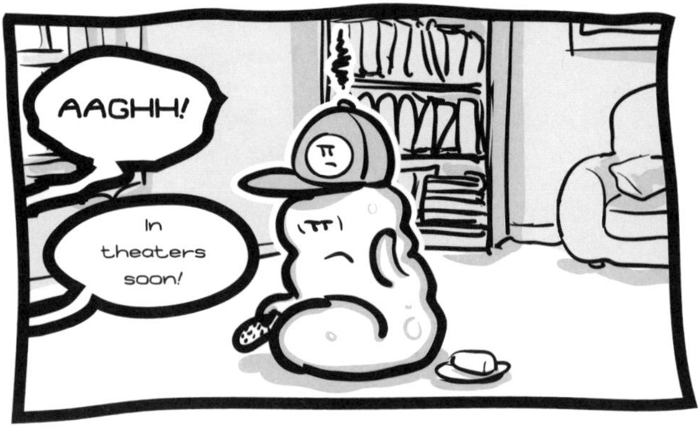
AAGHH!
In theaters soon!

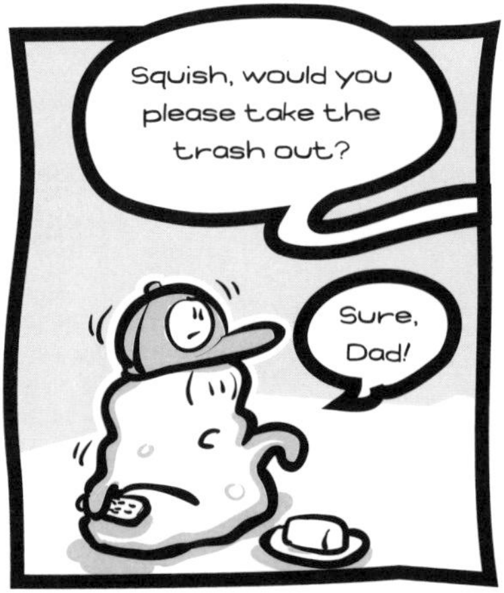
Squish, would you please take the trash out?
Sure, Dad!

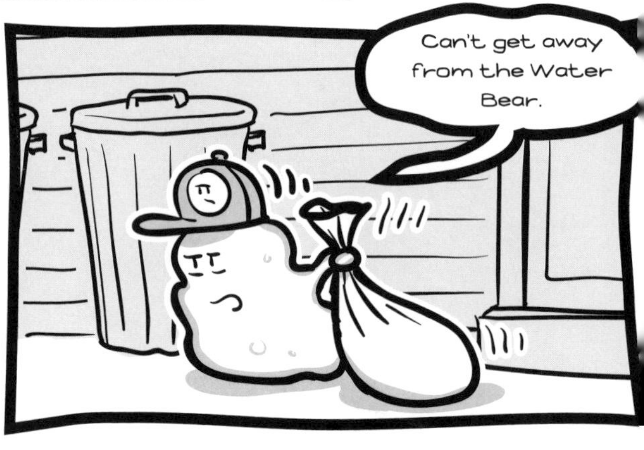
Can't get away from the Water Bear.

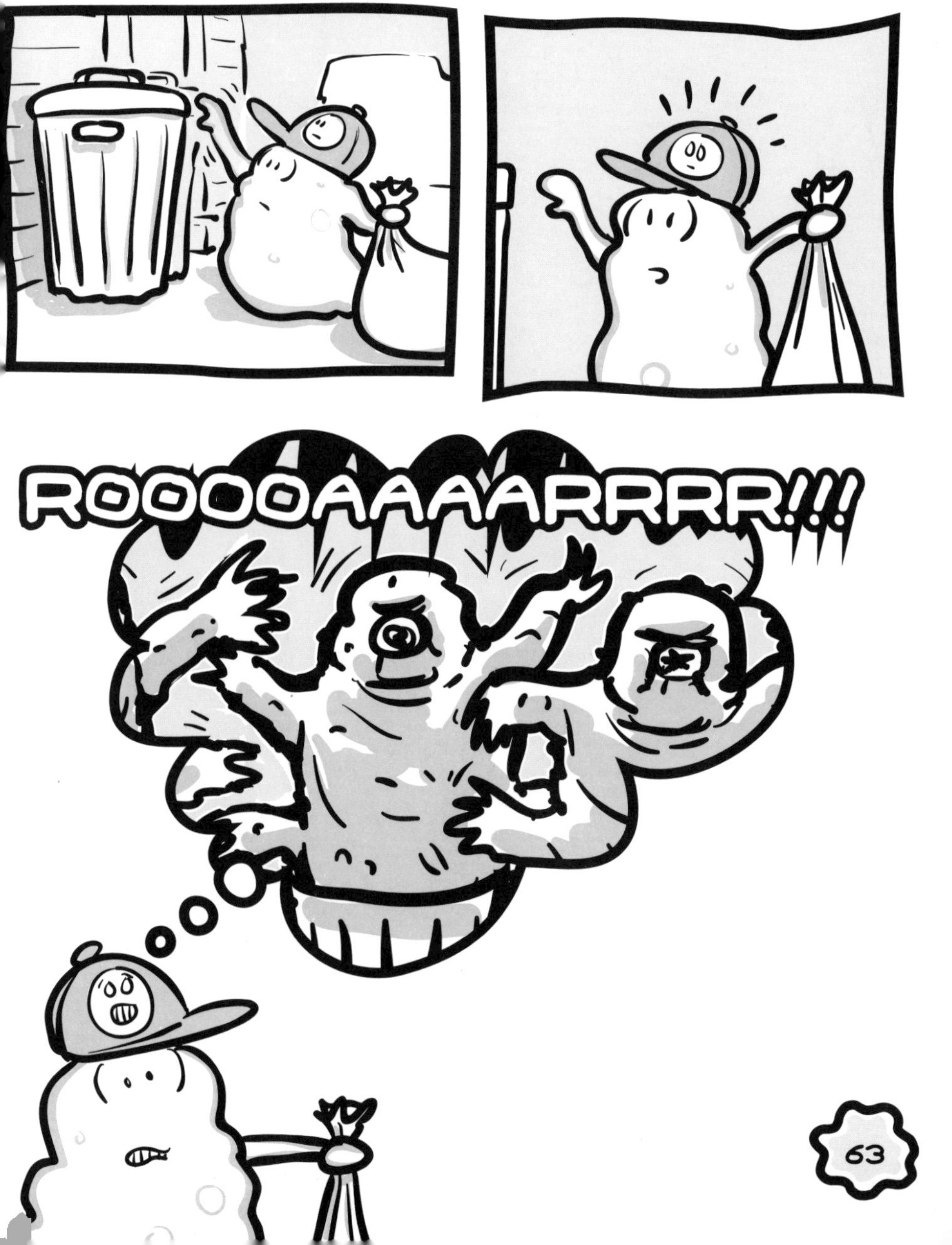
ROOOOAAAAARRRRR!!!

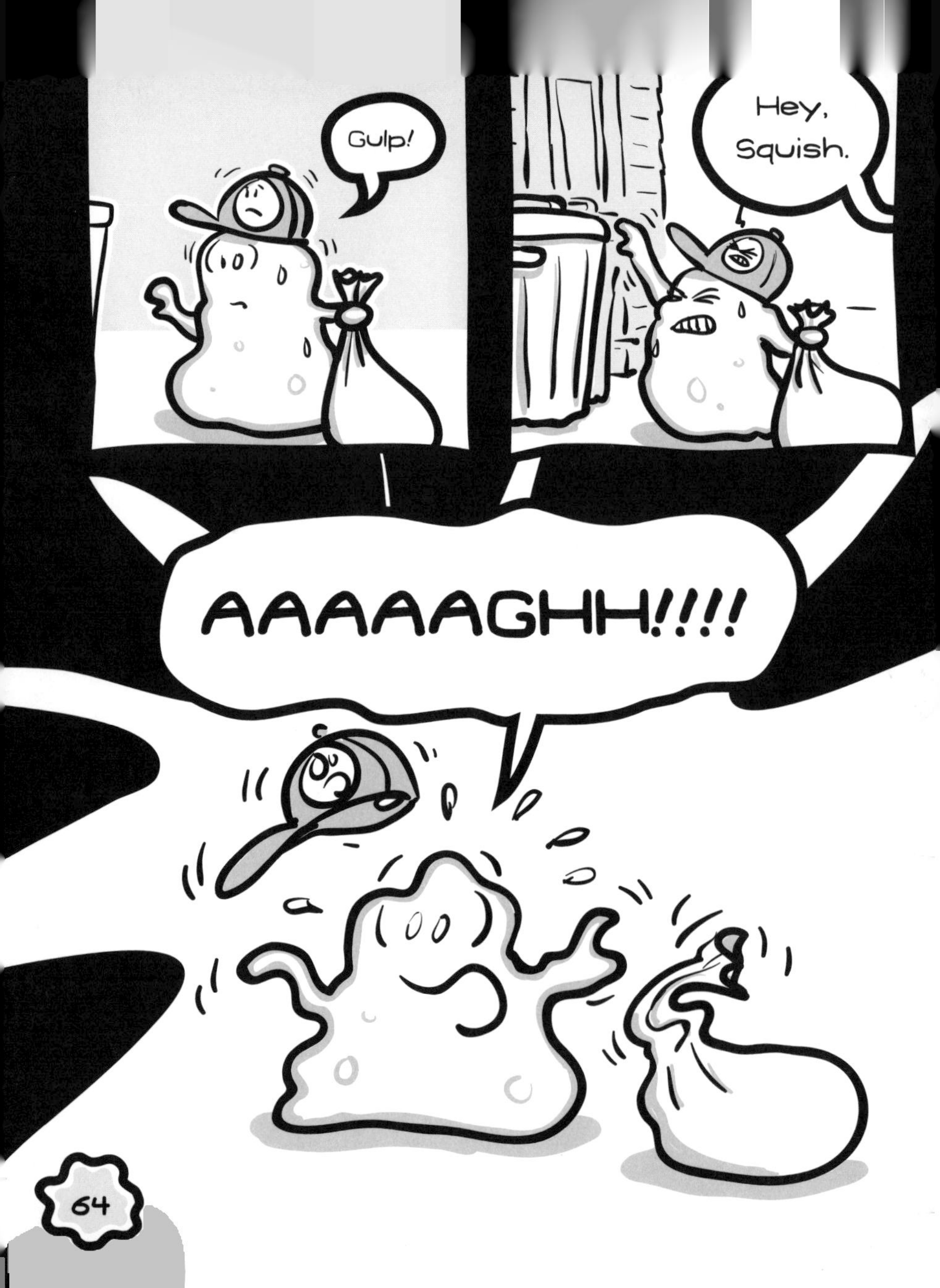
Gulp!
Hey, Squish.
AAAAAGHH!!!!

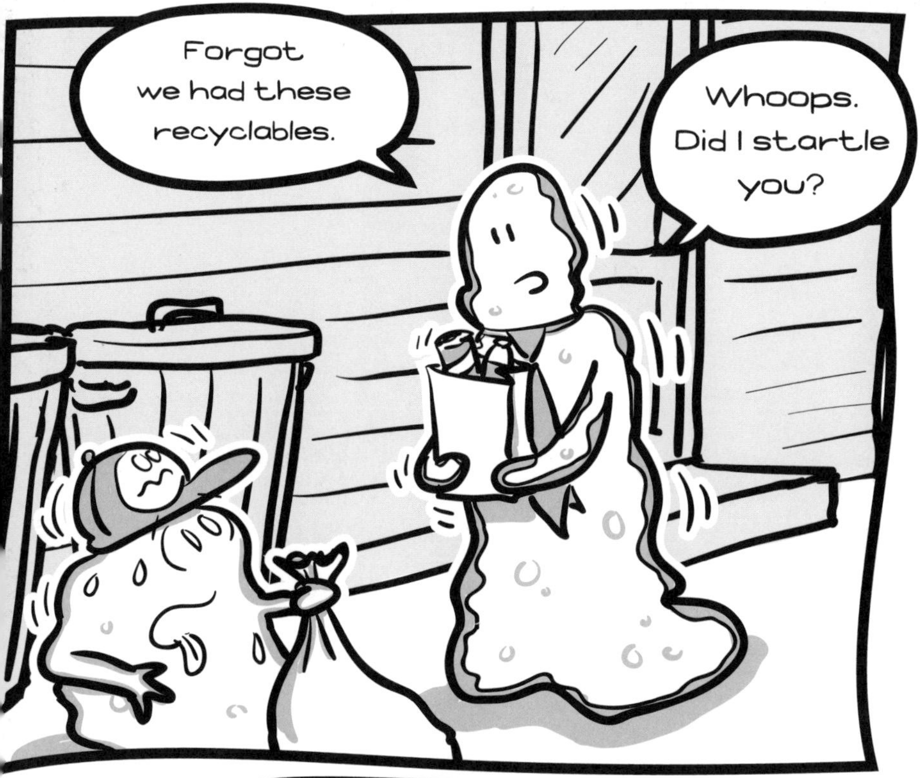
Forgot we had these recyclables.
Whoops. Did I startle you?

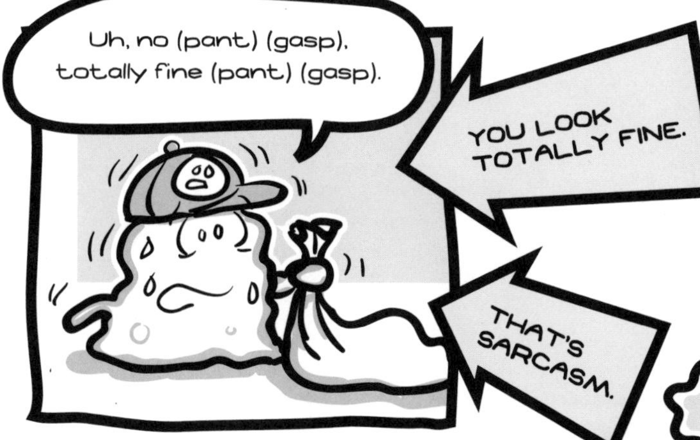
Uh, no (pant) (gasp), totally fine (pant) (gasp).
YOU LOOK TOTALLY FINE.
THAT'S SARCASM.

* TRUE SCIENTIFIC FACT: STINKY SOCKS ARE STINKY BECAUSE OF BACTERIA.

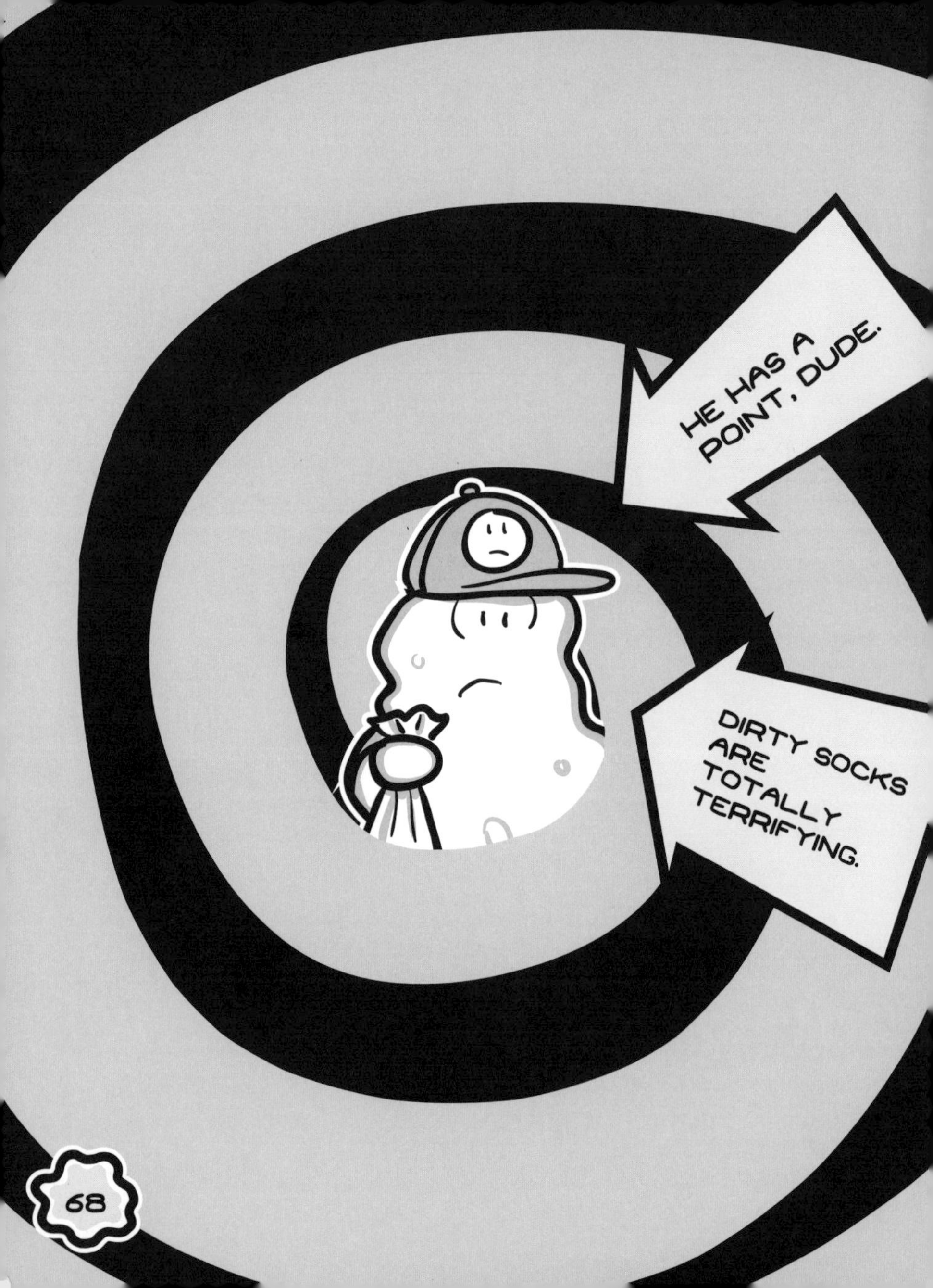
HE HAS A POINT, DUDE.
DIRTY SOCKS ARE TOTALLY TERRIFYING.

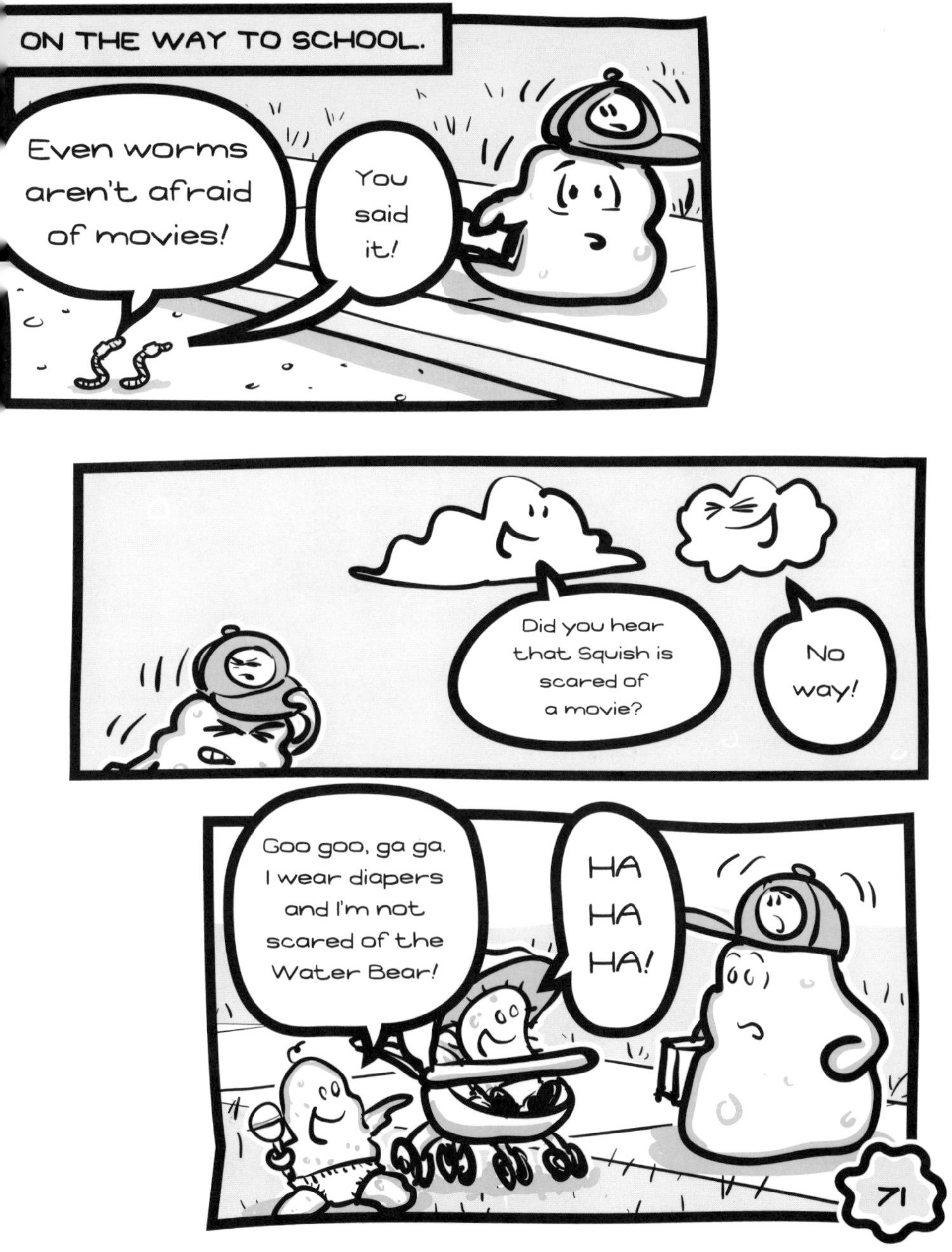

ON THE WAY TO SCHOOL.
Even worms aren't afraid of movies!
You said it!
Did you hear that Squish is scared of a movie?
No way!
Goo goo, ga ga. I wear diapers and I'm not scared of the Water Bear!
HA HA HA!

RED OF A MOVIE? I HEARD IT'S TRUE! BU
WATER BEAR ISN'T REAL! HECK, IT ISN
I ALL THAT SCARY! ONLY A SCAREDY-BAE
LD BE WORRIED ABOUT SOME DUMB OL
ER BEAR COMING AFTER YOU! HA HA H
A! DID YOU HEAR THAT SQUISH IS AFRAID (
E MUST BE A BABY. NO WAY! EVEN BABIE
I'T SCARED OF MOVIES LIKE THAT. WH
LITTLE SISTER SAW THE WATER BEA
E AND SHE WASN'T SCARED AT ALL. DOE
TILL TAKE NAPS? HA HA HA! I WONDE
E'S SCARED OF KITTENS AND RAINBOW
T HE IS! SCAREDY-CAT. HE'S PROBABL
H A SCAREDY-CAT THAT HE'S SCARE
ATS, TOO! HOW CAN HE BE SO TOTALL
E? LAME. SO, SO LAME. WHAT A BABY.
CARED OF FLOWERS? SCAREDY-CAT! HE
RED! WHAT A SCARED OF A MOV
SCAREDY SC ISH-SQUISH! HA H
A HA! SAD P MP. HOW OLD IS H
VAY? HE MU E IN KINDERGARTE
T'S NOT EVE MY BABY BRO ER
IDERGARTEN, AND HE ISN'T SCARED AN
E! HA HA HA! TOTALLY LAME.

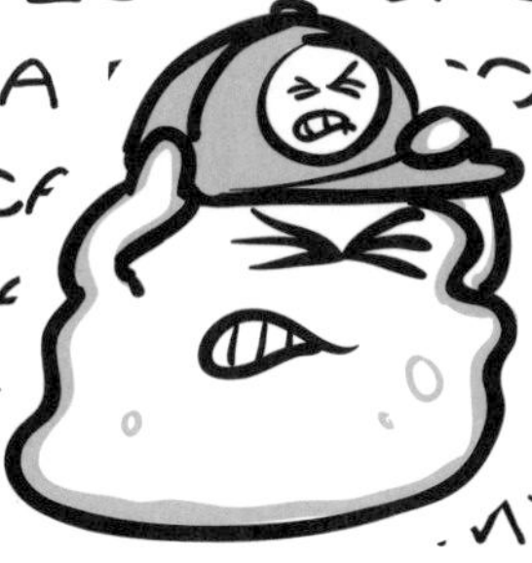

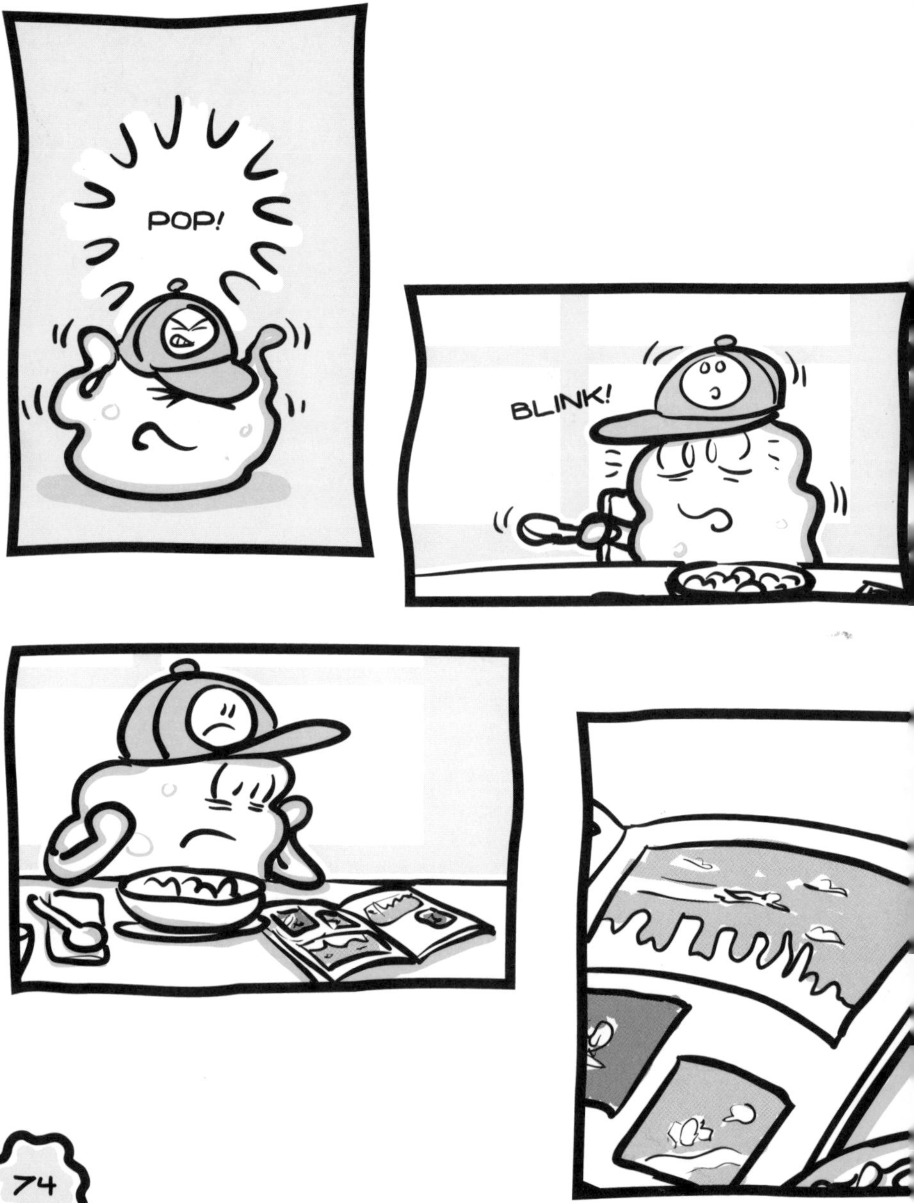
POP!
BLINK!

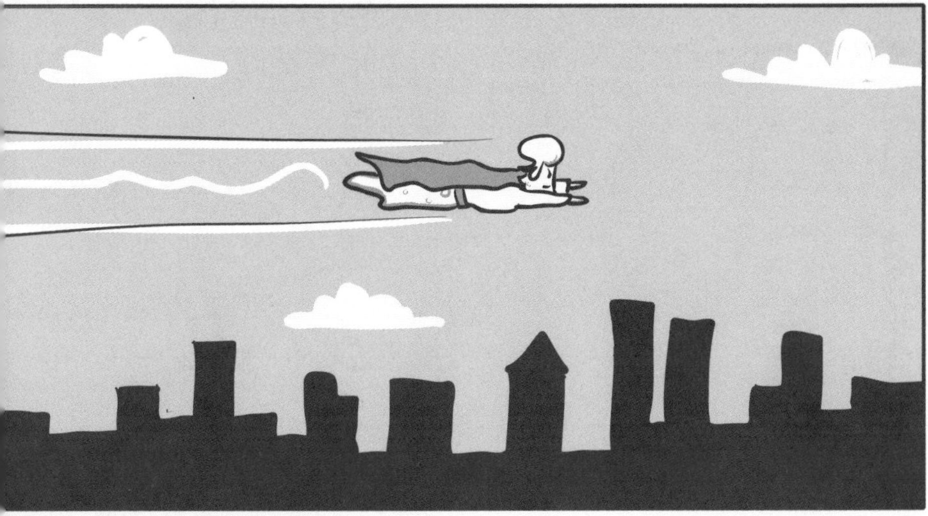

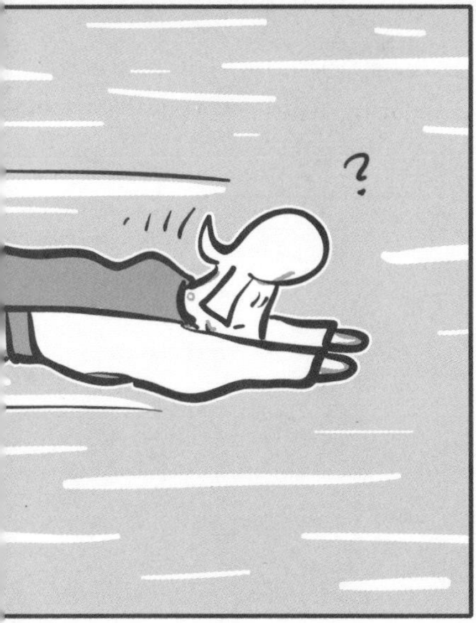
?

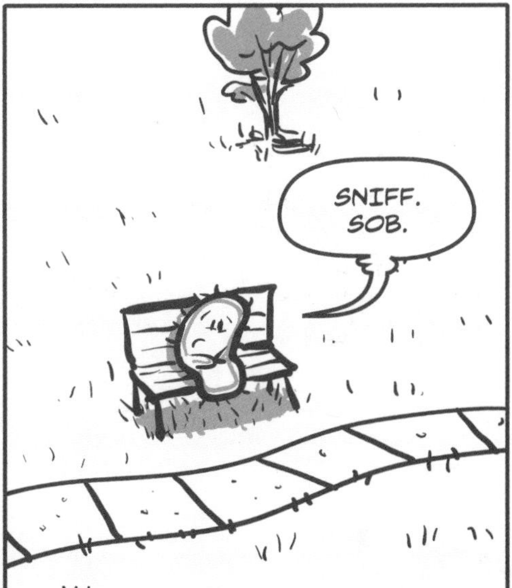
SNIFF.
SOB.

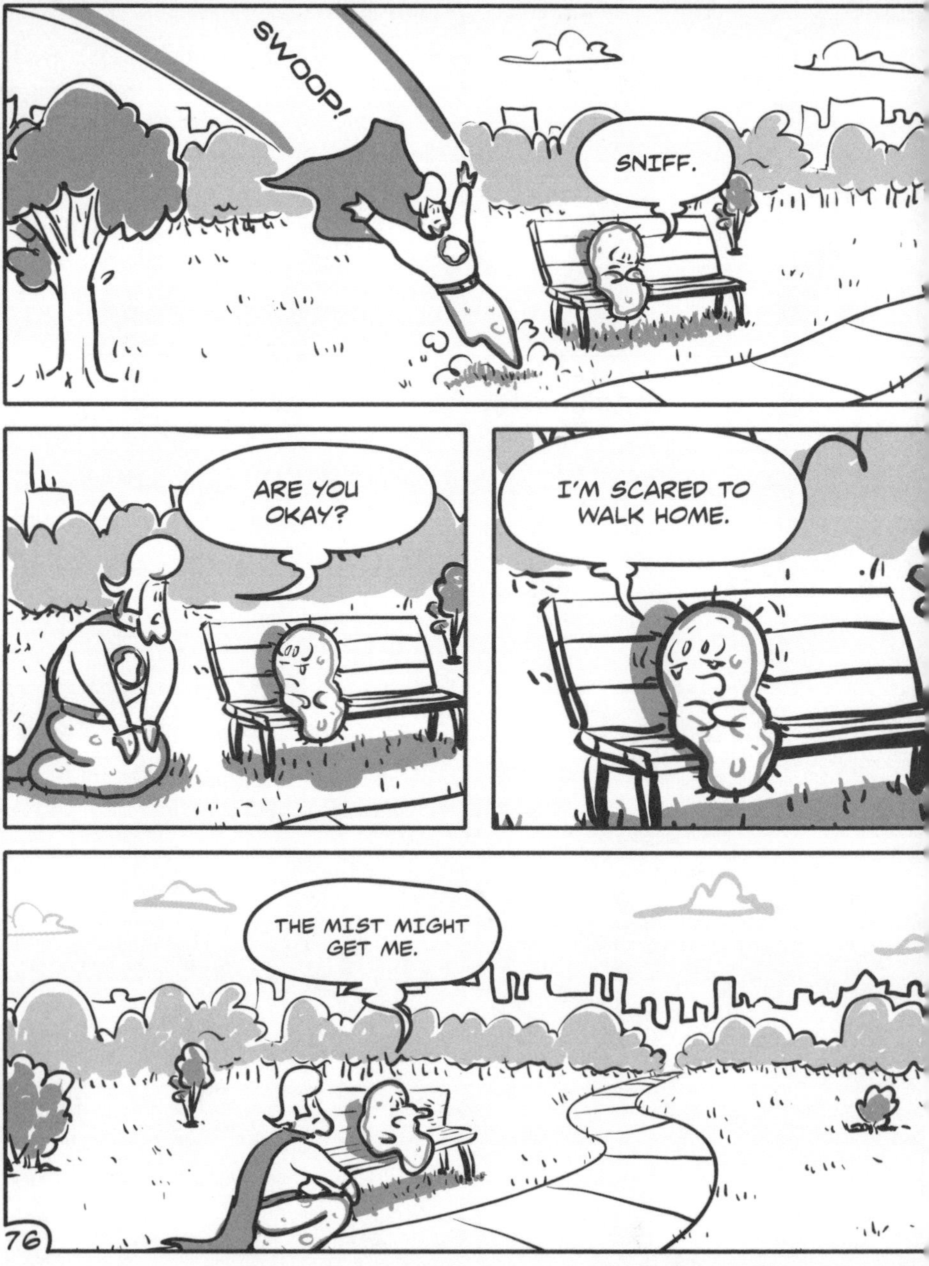
SWOOP!
SNIFF.
ARE YOU OKAY?
I'M SCARED TO WALK HOME.
THE MIST MIGHT GET ME.

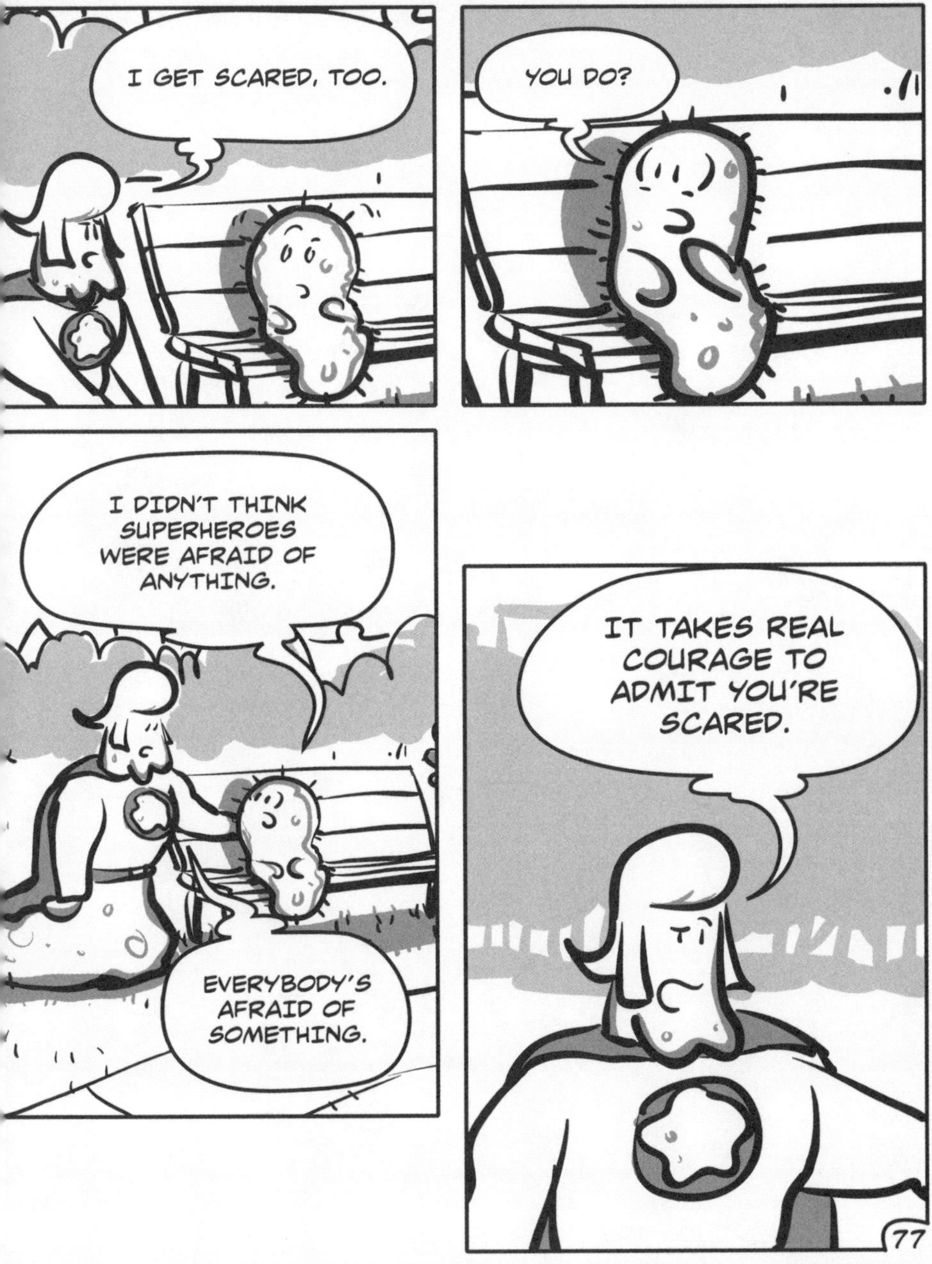
I GET SCARED, TOO.
YOU DO?
I DIDN'T THINK SUPERHEROES WERE AFRAID OF ANYTHING.
EVERYBODY'S AFRAID OF SOMETHING.
IT TAKES REAL COURAGE TO ADMIT YOU'RE SCARED.

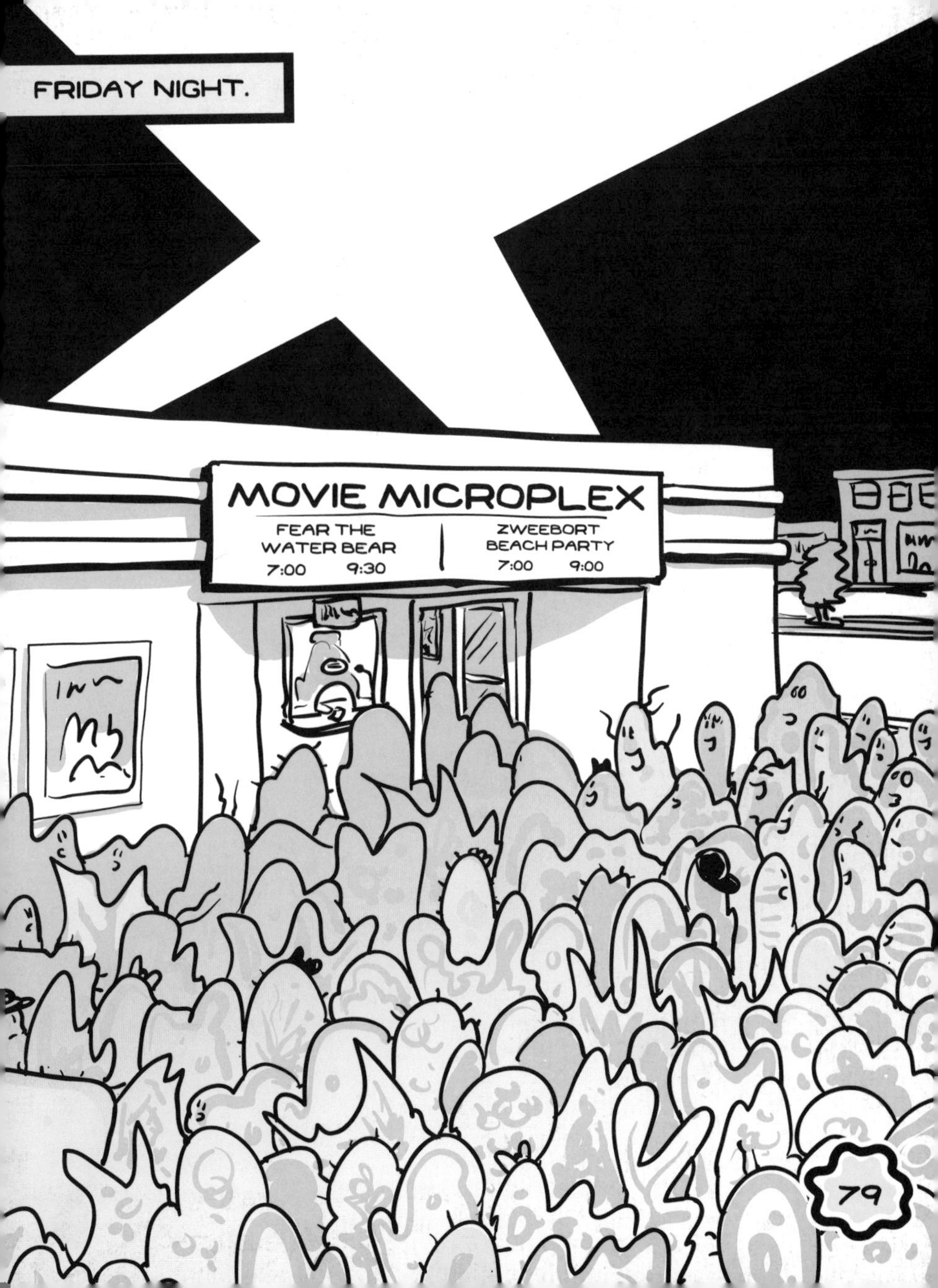
FRIDAY NIGHT.
MOVIE MICROPLEX
FEAR THE WATER BEAR 7:00 9:30
ZWEEBORT BEACH PARTY 7:00 9:00

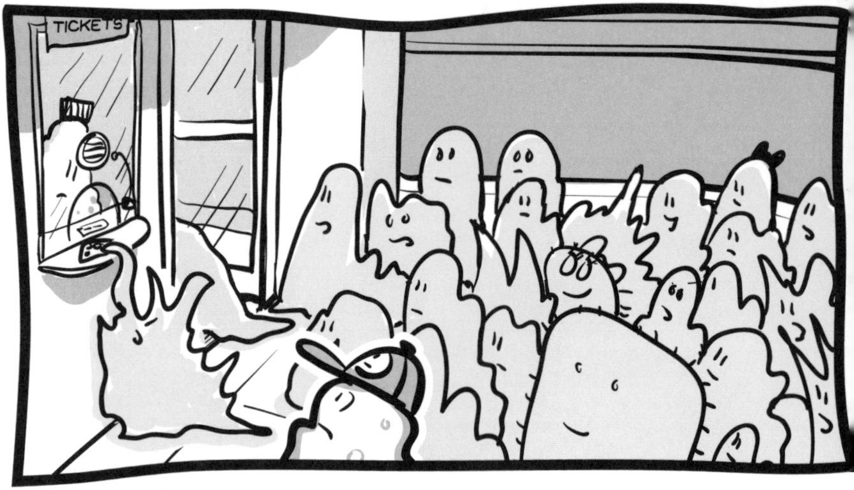
TICKETS

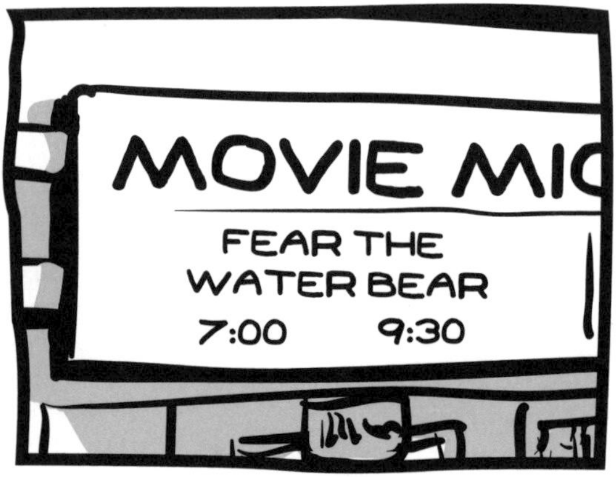
MOVIE MIC
FEAR THE
WATER BEAR
7:00 9:30

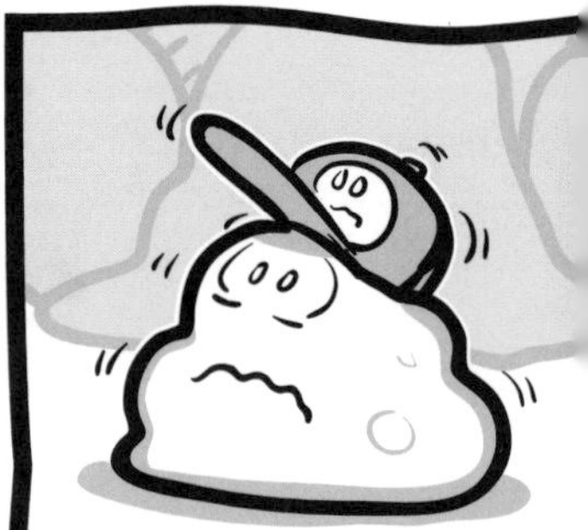

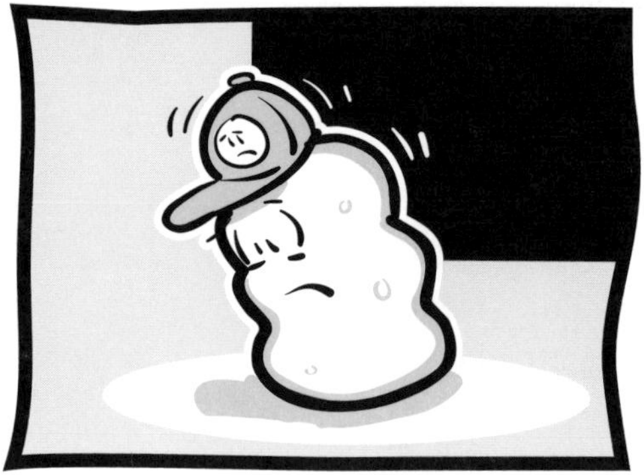

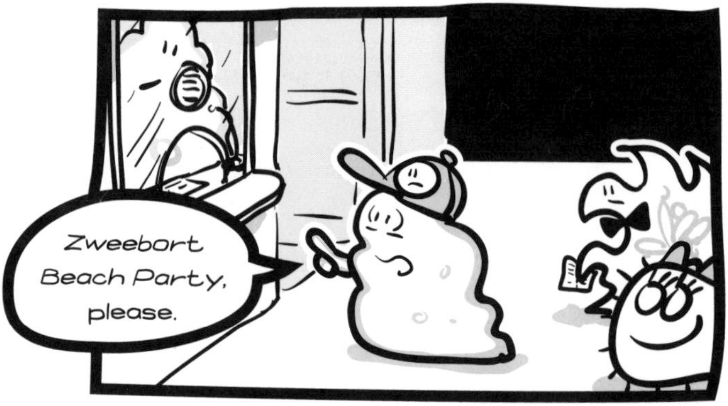
Zweebort Beach Party, please.

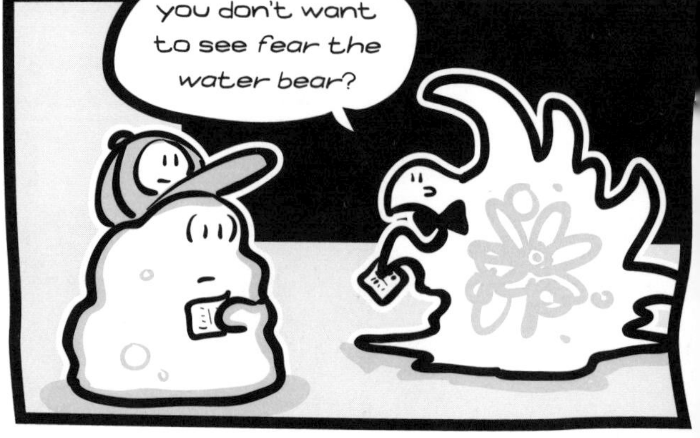
you don't want to see *fear the water bear*?

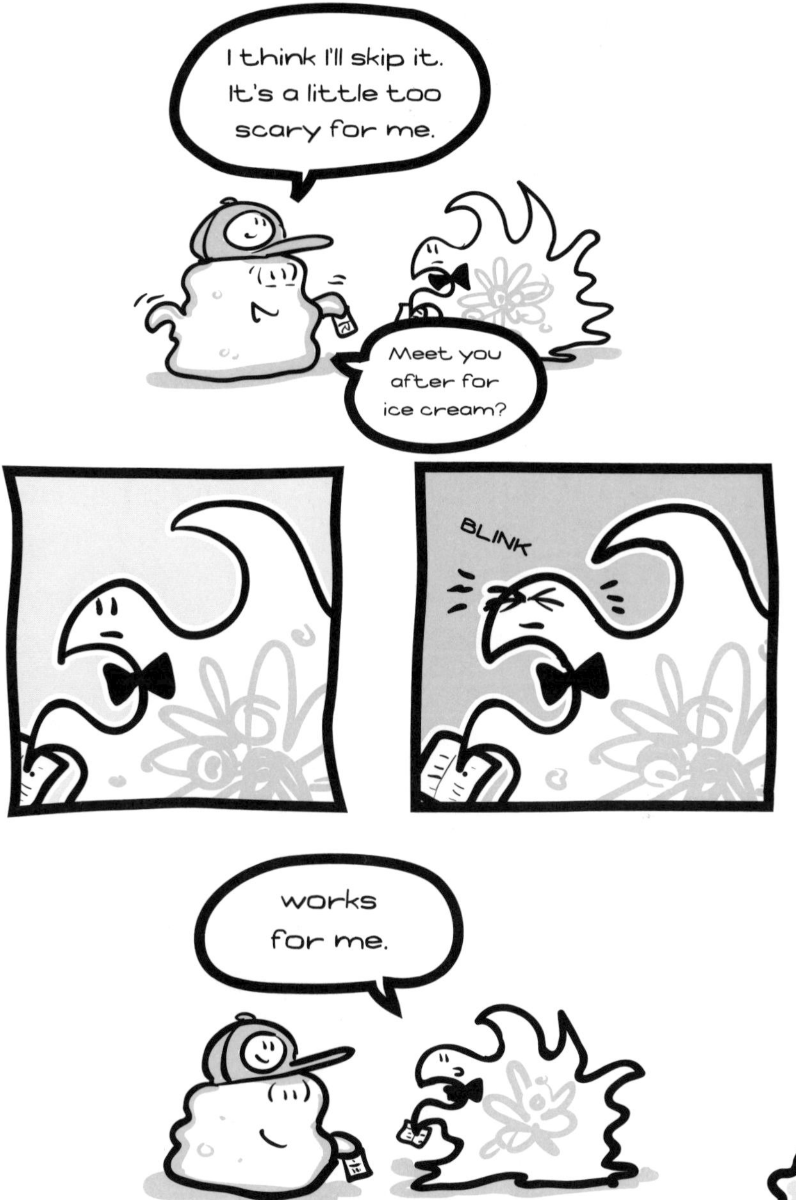
I think I'll skip it. It's a little too scary for me.
Meet you after for ice cream?
BLINK
works for me.

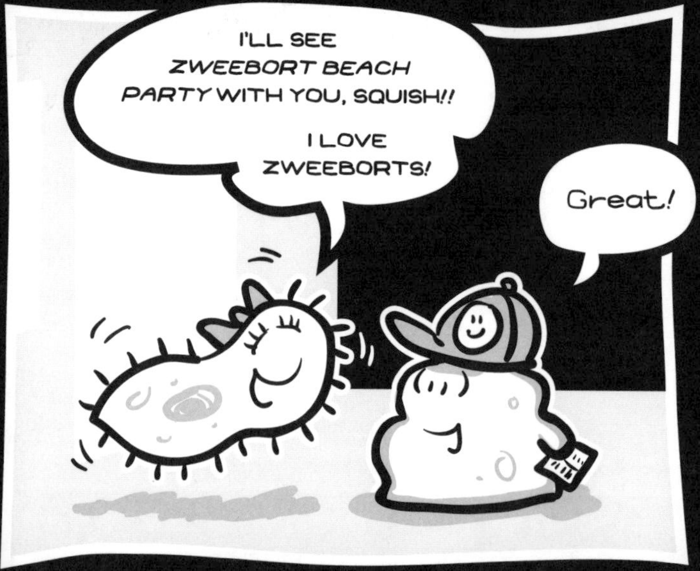
I'LL SEE ZWEEBORT BEACH PARTY WITH YOU, SQUISH!!
I LOVE ZWEEBORTS!
Great!

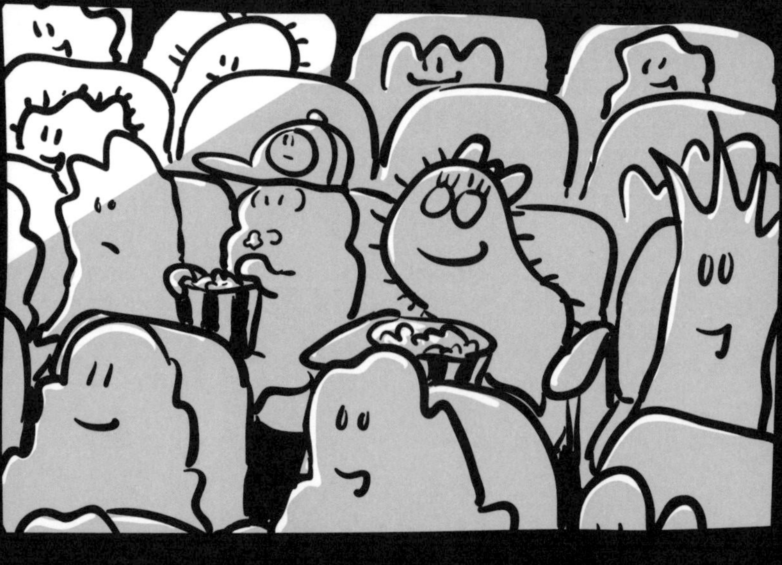

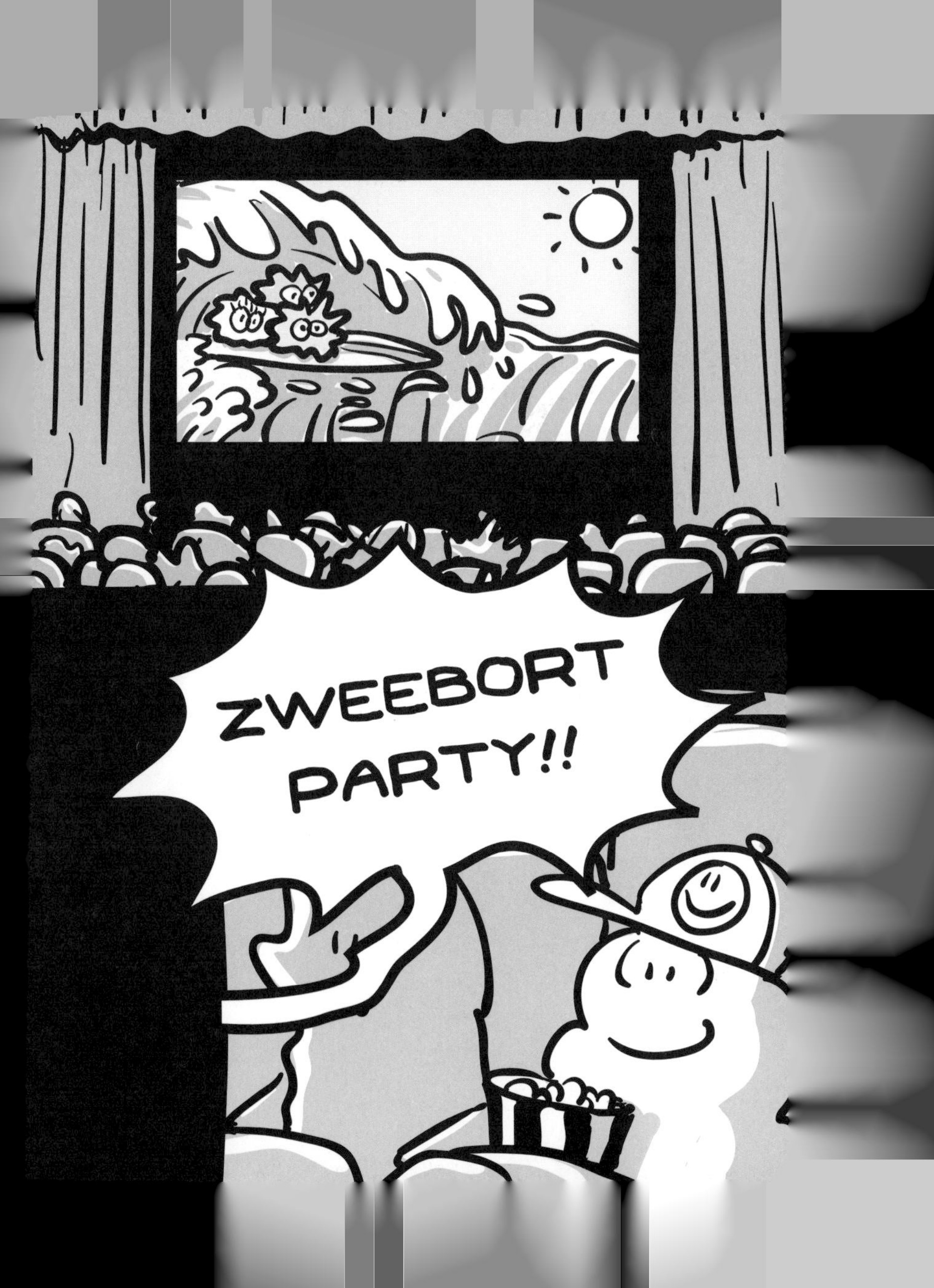
ZWEEBORT PARTY!!

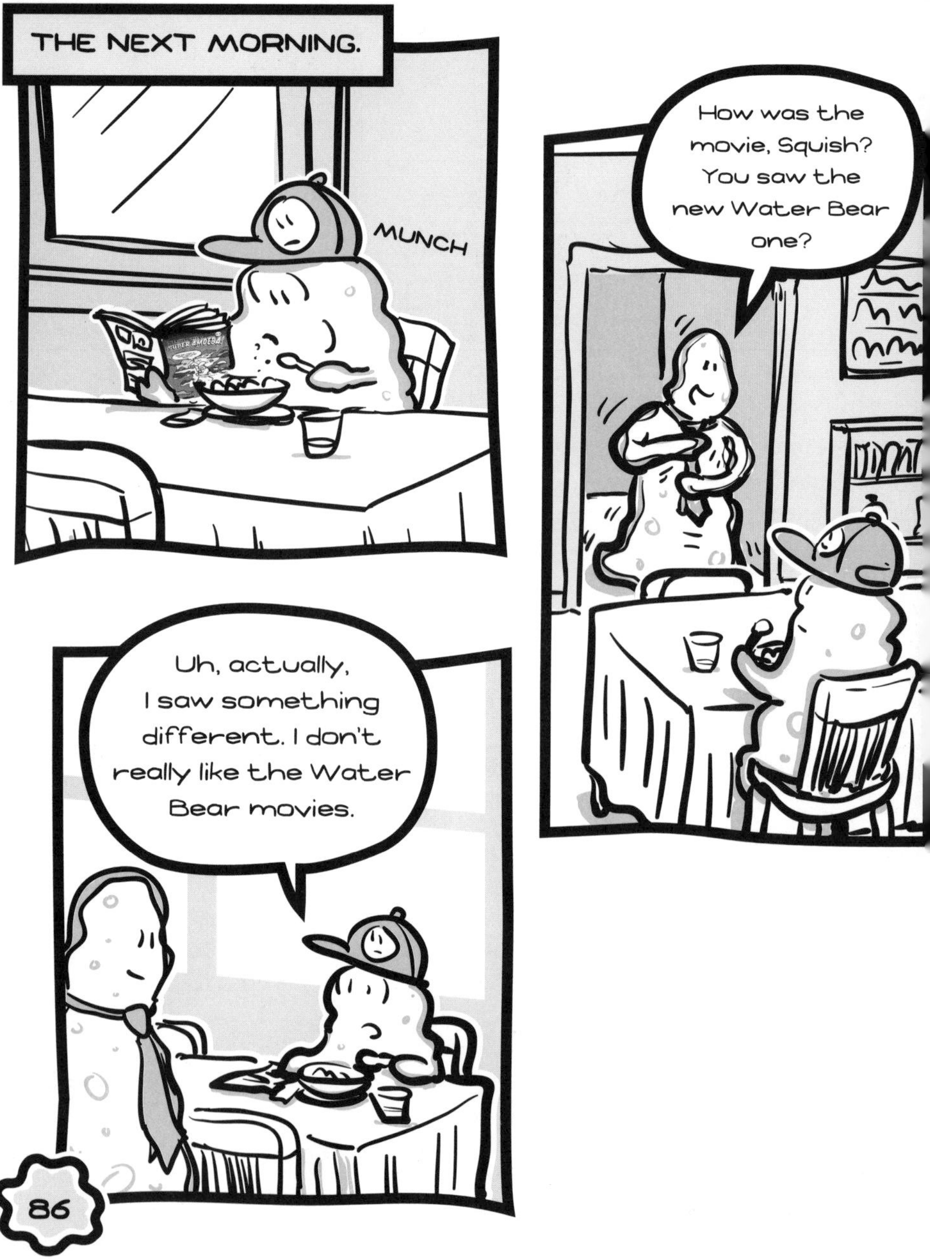
THE NEXT MORNING.
MUNCH
How was the movie, Squish? You saw the new Water Bear one?
Uh, actually, I saw something different. I don't really like the Water Bear movies.

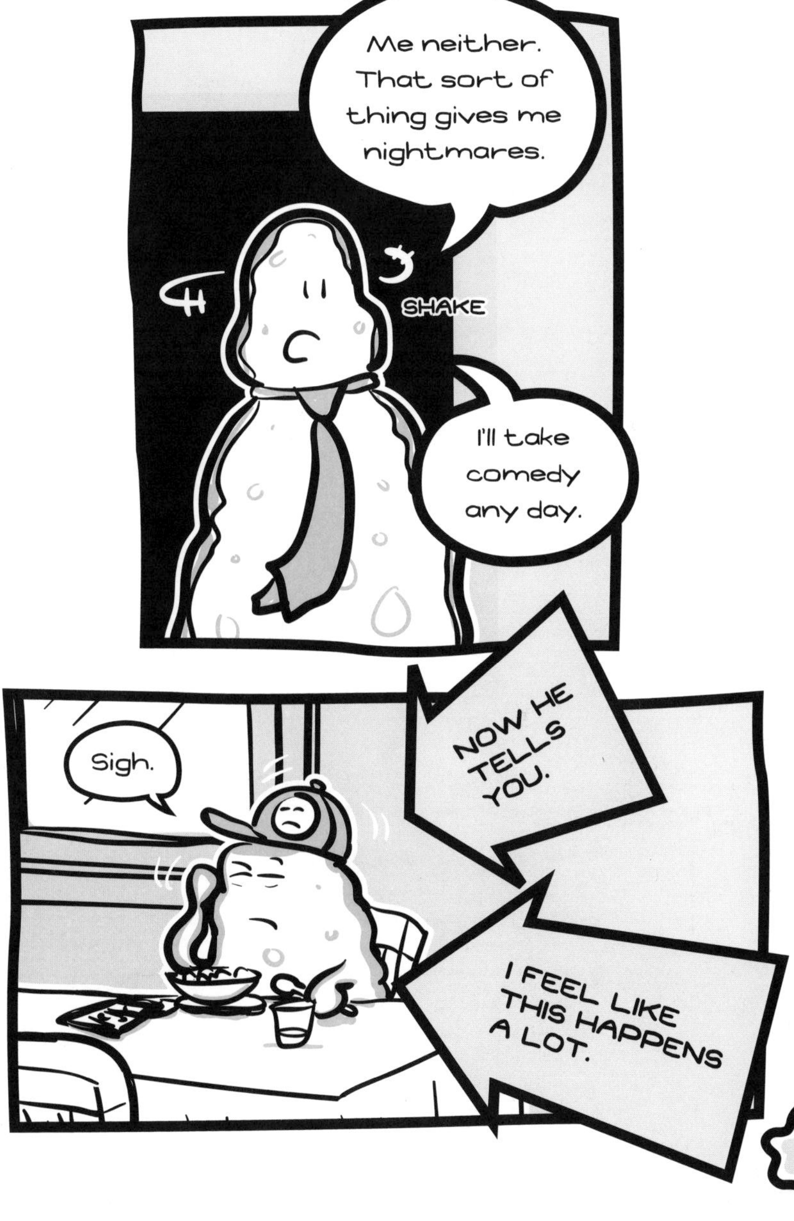
Me neither. That sort of thing gives me nightmares.
SHAKE
I'll take comedy any day.
Sigh.
NOW HE TELLS YOU.
I FEEL LIKE THIS HAPPENS A LOT.

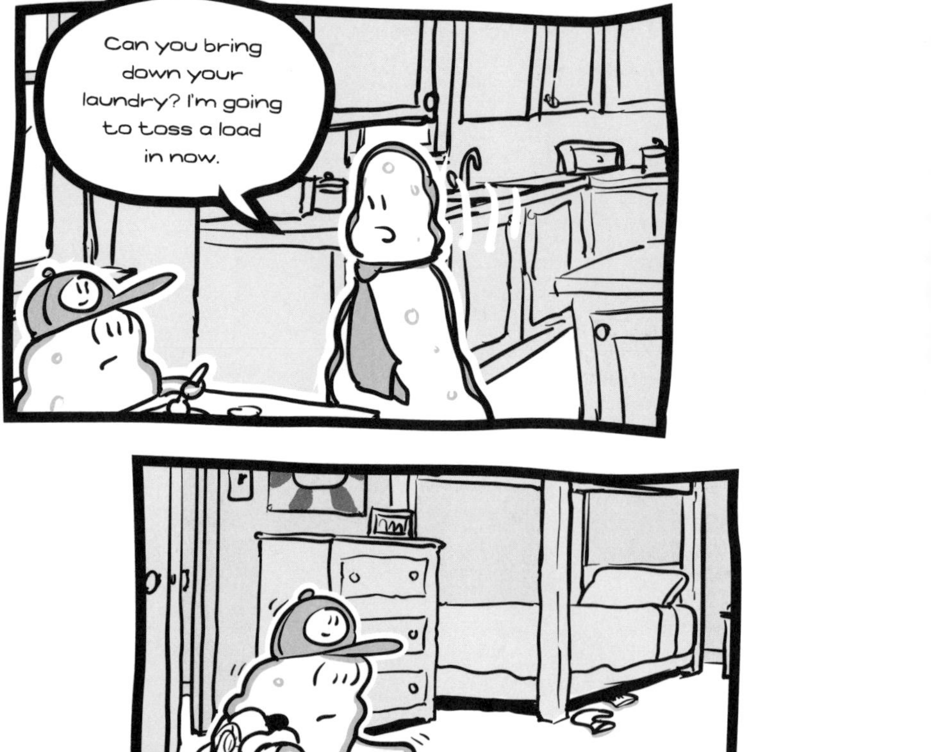
Can you bring down your laundry? I'm going to toss a load in now.

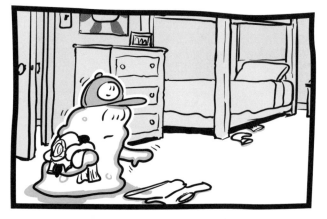

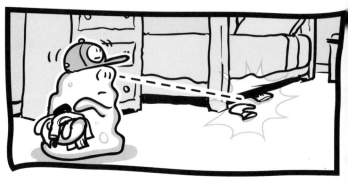

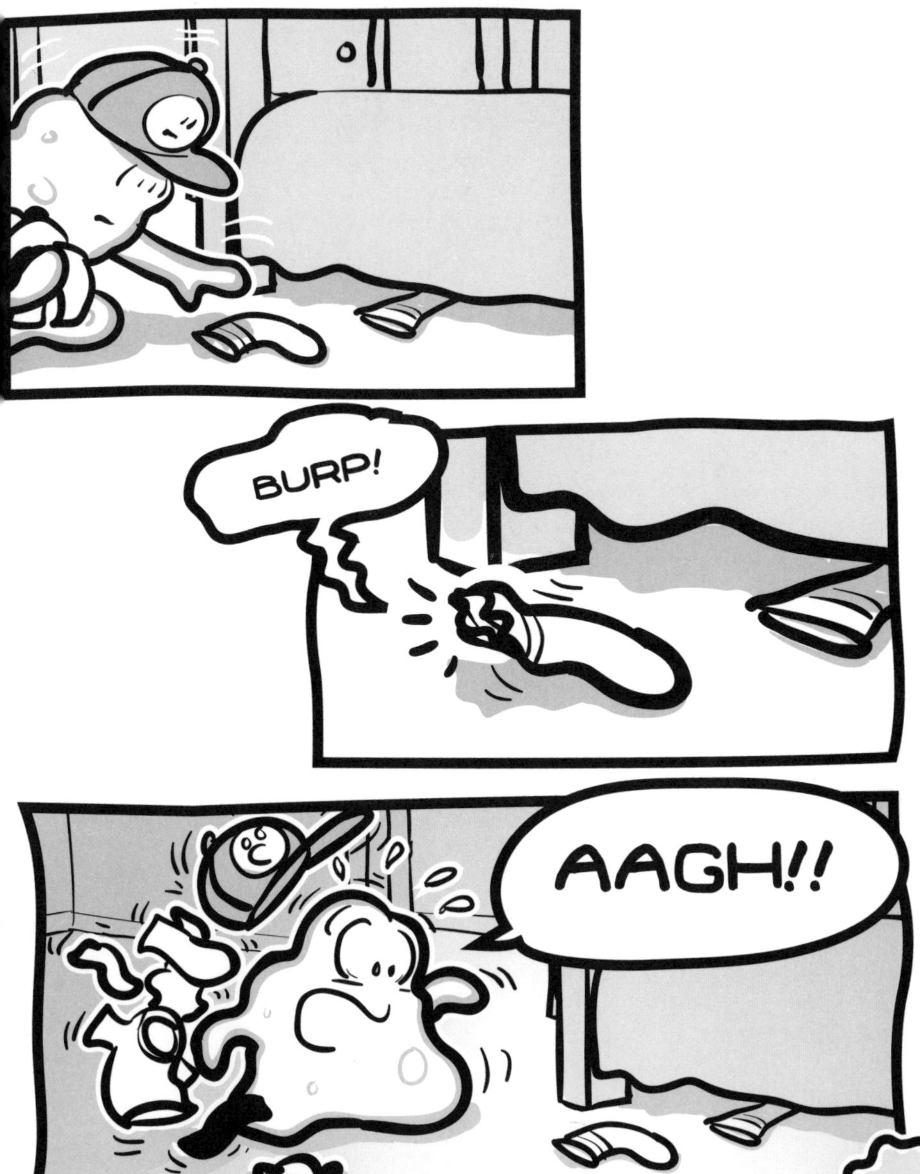
BURP!
AAGH!!

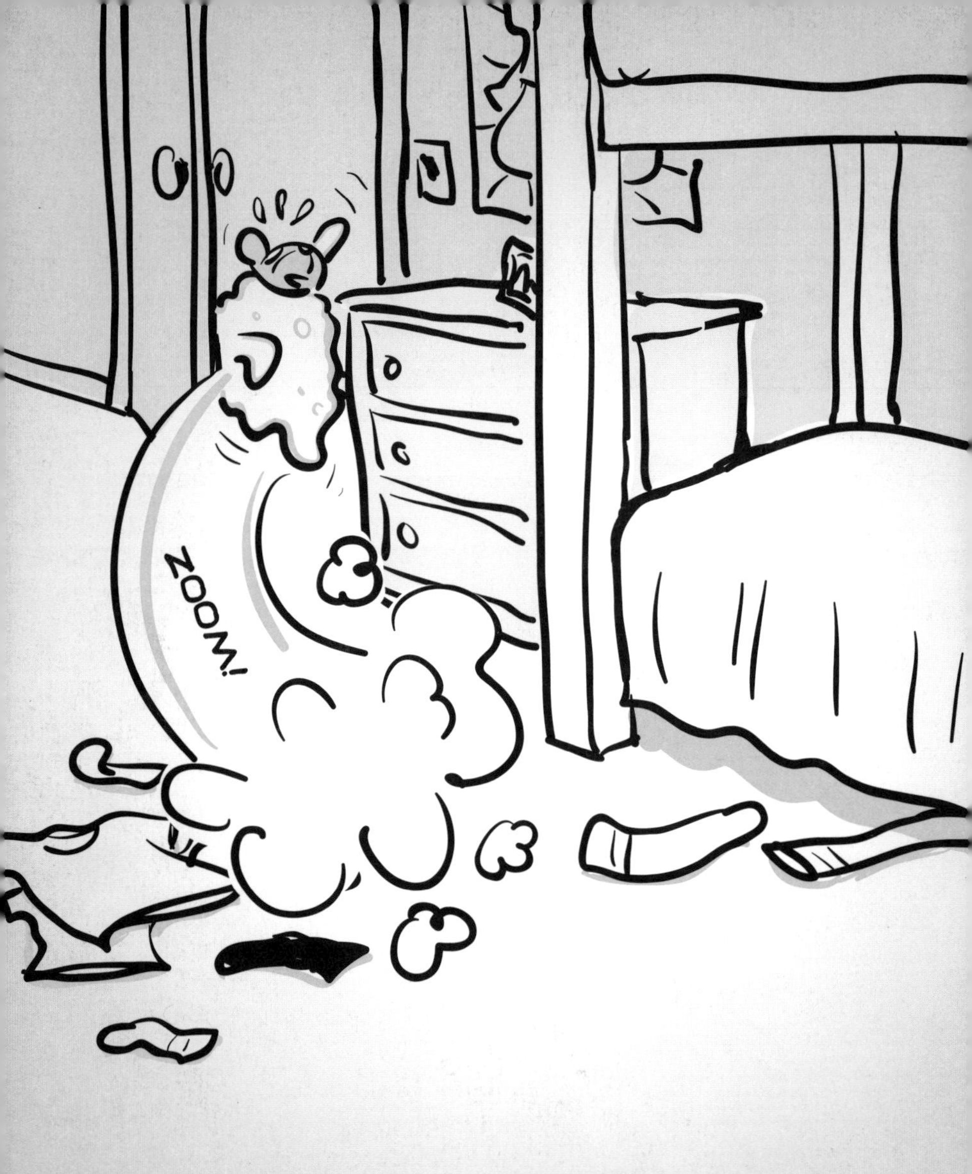
ZOOM!

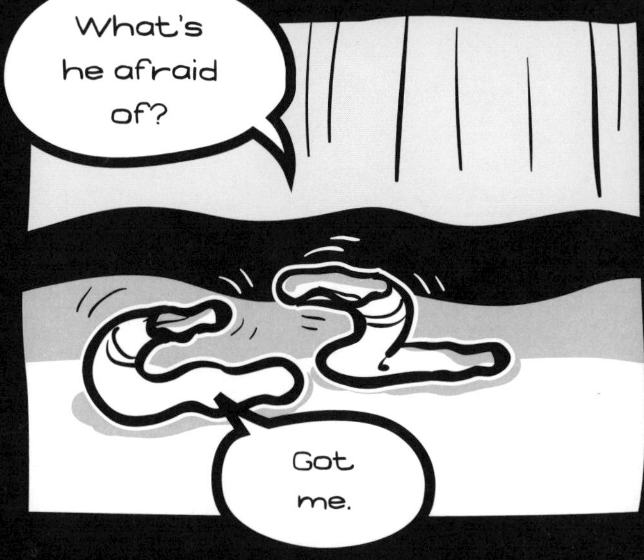
What's he afraid of?
Got me.

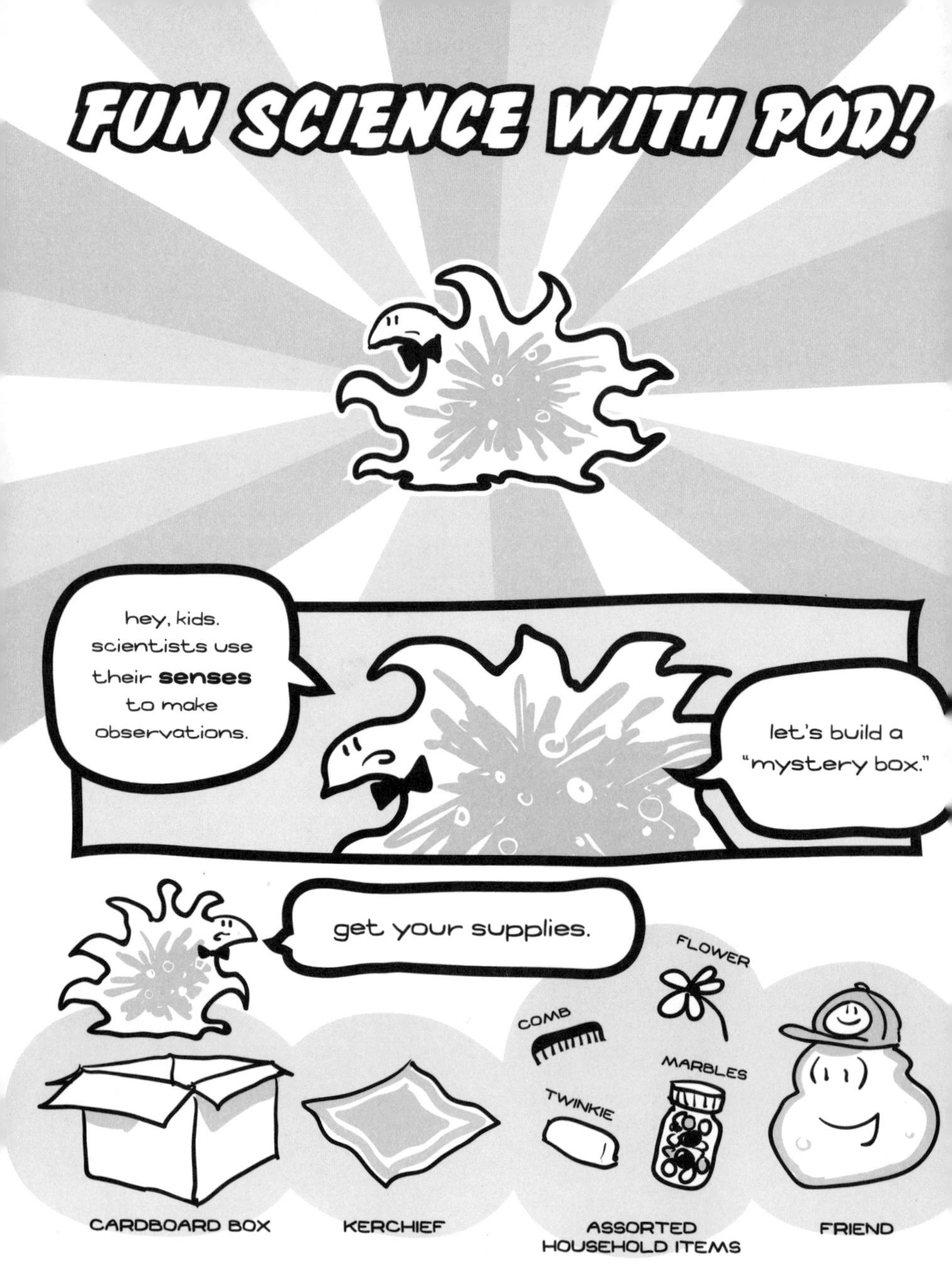
FUN SCIENCE WITH POD!
hey, kids. scientists use their **senses** to make observations.
let's build a "mystery box."
get your supplies.
FLOWER
COMB
MARBLES
TWINKIE
CARDBOARD BOX
KERCHIEF
ASSORTED HOUSEHOLD ITEMS
FRIEND

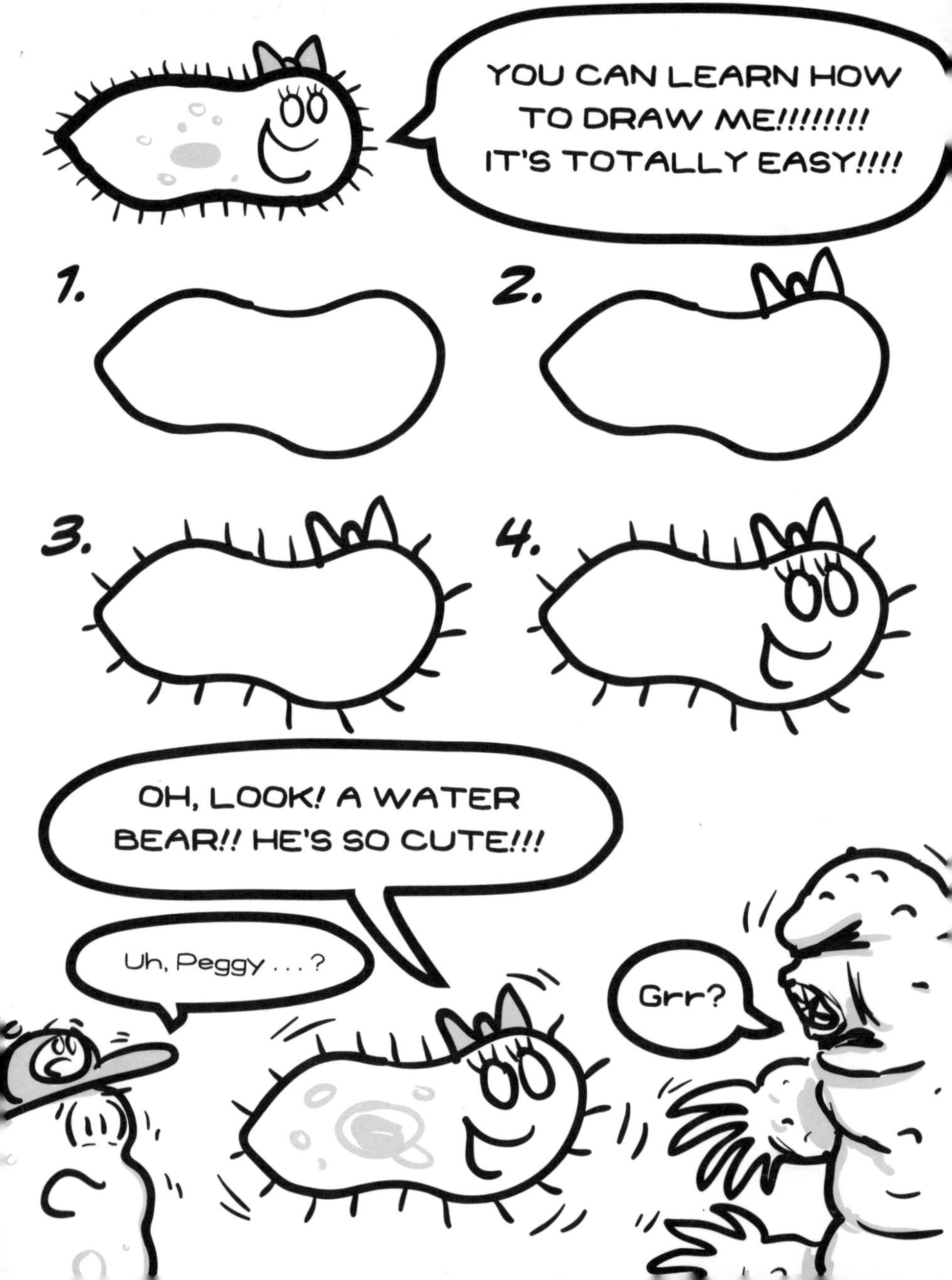
YOU CAN LEARN HOW TO DRAW ME!!!!!!!!! IT'S TOTALLY EASY!!!!
1.
2.
3.
4.
OH, LOOK! A WATER BEAR!! HE'S SO CUTE!!!
Uh, Peggy . . . ?
Grr?

IF YOU LIKE SQUISH, YOU'LL LOVE BABYMOUSE!

#1 BABYMOUSE: Queen of the World!

#2 BABYMOUSE: Our Hero

#3 BABYMOUSE: Beach Babe

#4 BABYMOUSE: Rock Star

#5 BABYMOUSE: Heartbreaker

#6 CAMP BABYMOUSE

#7 BABYMOUSE: Skater Girl

#8 BABYMOUSE: Puppy Love

#9 BABYMOUSE: Monster Mash

#10 BABYMOUSE: The Musical

#11 BABYMOUSE: Dragonslayer

#12 BABYMOUSE: Burns Rubber

#13 BABYMOUSE: Cupcake Tycoon

#14 BABYMOUSE: Mad Scientist

#15 A Very BABYMOUSE Christmas

#16 BABYMOUSE for President

#17 Extreme BABYMOUSE

#18 Happy Birthday, BABYMOUSE

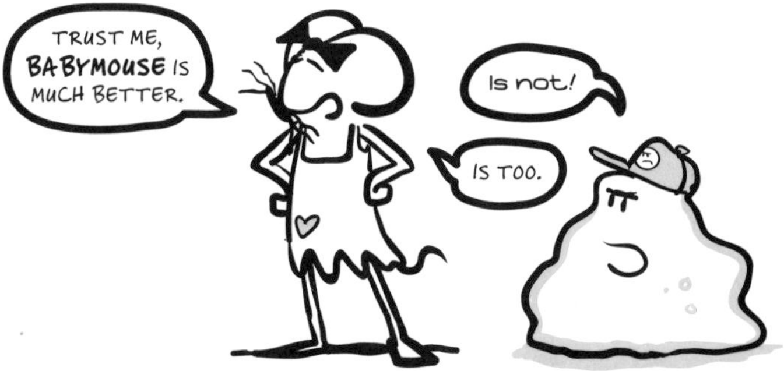
TRUST ME, BABYMOUSE IS MUCH BETTER.
Is not!
IS TOO.

Look for these other great books
by Jennifer L. Holm!

THE BOSTON JANE TRILOGY
EIGHTH GRADE IS MAKING ME SICK
MIDDLE SCHOOL IS WORSE THAN MEATLOAF
OUR ONLY MAY AMELIA
PENNY FROM HEAVEN
TURTLE IN PARADISE

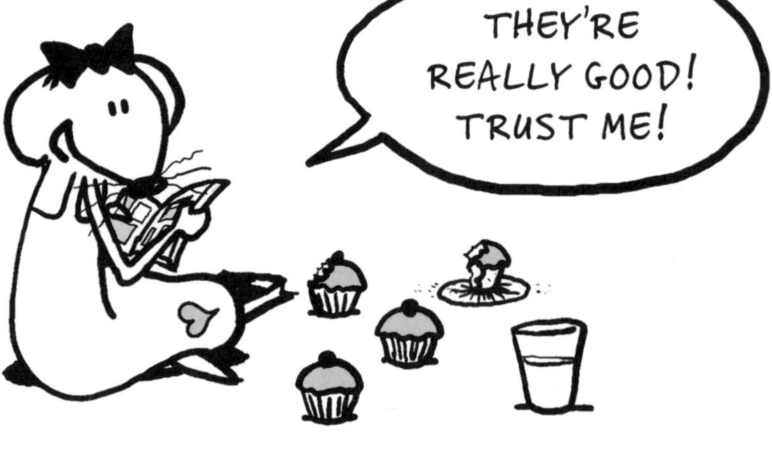
THEY'RE REALLY GOOD! TRUST ME!